WORDS OF GLORY

I0639701

WORDS OF GLORY
INSPIRING SPEECHES FROM THE GREATEST LEADERS

RUPA

This is a Print On Demand copy and hence does not have special finishing on the cover.

Published by
Rupa Publications India Pvt. Ltd 2019
7/16, Ansari Road, Daryaganj
New Delhi 110002

Sales centres:
Allahabad Bengaluru Chennai
Hyderabad Jaipur Kathmandu
Kolkata Mumbai

Copyright © Rupa Publications India Pvt. Ltd 2019

All rights reserved.
No part of this publication may be reproduced, transmitted,
or stored in a retrieval system, in any form or by any means,
electronic, mechanical, photocopying, recording or otherwise,
without the prior permission of the publisher.

ISBN - 978-93-5333-354-6

First impression 2019

10 9 8 7 6 5 4 3 2 1

The moral right of the author has been asserted.

This book is sold subject to the condition that it shall not, by way
of trade or otherwise, be lent, resold, hired out, or otherwise circulated,
without the publisher's prior consent, in any form of binding
or cover other than that in which it is published.

Contents

1

Alexander the Great

*'Come, then: add the rest of Asia
to what you already possess.'*

∿

*This speech was given in 326 BC at the Hydaspes River
in India by Alexander the Great. Prior to this speech,
Alexander and his army had been fighting for ten years.
Alexander and his men were undefeated and had
captured Egypt, Greece and the former Persian Empire.
This speech was meant to encourage his army to carry on.*

From the Campaigns of Alexander

Banks of the Hydaspes (Jhelum)
326 BC

I observe, gentlemen, that when I would lead you on a new
venture you no longer follow me with your old spirit. I have

asked you to meet me that we may come to a decision together: are we, upon my advice, to go forward, or, upon yours, to turn back?

If you have any complaint to make about the results of your efforts hitherto, or about myself as your commander, there is no more to say. But let me remind you: through your courage and endurance you have gained possession of Ionia, the Hellespont, both Phrygias, Cappadocia, Paphlagonia, Lydia, Caria, Lycia, Pamphylia, Phoenicia, and Egypt; the Greek part of Libya is now yours, together with much of Arabia, lowland Syria, Mesopotamia, Babylon and Susia; Persia and Media with all the territories either formerly controlled by them or not are in your hands; you have made yourselves masters of the lands beyond the Caspian Gates, beyond the Caucasus, beyond the Tanais, of Bactria, Hyrcania, and the Hyrcanian sea; we have driven the Scythians back into the desert; and Indus and Hydaspes, Acesines and Hydraotes flow now through country which is ours. With all that accomplished, why do you hesitate to extend the power of Macedon—your power—to the Hyphasis and the tribes on the other side? Are you afraid that a few natives who may still be left will offer opposition? Come, come! These natives either surrender without a blow or are caught on the run—or leave their country undefended for your taking; and when we take it, we make a present of it to those who have joined us of their own free will and fight on our side.

For a man who is a man, work, in my belief, if it

is directed to noble ends, has no object beyond itself; nonetheless, if any of you wish to know what limit may be set to this particular campaign, let me tell you that the area of country still ahead of us, from here to the Ganges and the eastern ocean, is comparatively small. You will undoubtedly find that this ocean is connected with the Hyrcanian Sea, for the great Stream of Ocean encircles the earth. Moreover I shall prove to you, my friends, that the Indian and Persian Gulfs and the Hyrcanian Sea are all three connected and continuous. Our ships will sail round from the Persian Gulf to Libya as far as the Pillars of Hercules, whence all Libya to the eastward will soon be ours, and all Asia too, and to this empire there will be no boundaries but what God Himself has made for the whole world.

But if you turn back now, there will remain unconquered many warlike people between the Hyphasis and the Eastern Ocean, and many more to the northward and the Hyrcanian Sea, with the Scythians, too, not far away; so that if we withdraw now there is a danger that the territory which we do not yet securely hold may be stirred to revolt by some nation or other we have not yet forced into submission. Should that happen, all that we have done and suffered will have proved fruitless—or we shall be faced with the task of doing it over again from the beginning. Gentlemen of Macedon, and you, my friends and allies, this must not be. Stand firm; for well you know that hardship and danger are the price of glory, and that sweet is the savour of a life of courage and of deathless renown beyond the grave.

Are you not aware that if Heracles, my ancestor, had gone no further than Tiryns or Argos—or even than the Peloponnese or Thebes—he could never have won the glory which changed him from a man into a god, actual or apparent? Even Dionysus, who is a god indeed, in a sense beyond what is applicable to Heracles, faced not a few laborious tasks; yet we have done more: we have passed beyond Nysa and we have taken the rock of Aornos which Heracles himself could not take. Come, then; add the rest of Asia to what you already possess—a small addition to the great sum of your conquests. What great or noble work could we ourselves have achieved had we thought it enough, living at ease in Macedon, merely to guard our homes, accepting no burden beyond checking the encroachment of the Thracians on our borders, or the Illyrians and Triballians, or perhaps such Greeks as might prove a menace to our comfort?

I could not have blamed you for being the first to lose heart if I, your commander, had not shared in your exhausting marches and your perilous campaigns; it would have been natural enough if you had done all the work merely for others to reap the reward. But it is not so. You and I, gentlemen, have shared the labour and shared the danger, and the rewards are for us all. The conquered territory belongs to you; from your ranks the governors of it are chosen; already the greater part of its treasure passes into your hands, and when all Asia is overrun, then indeed I will go further than the mere satisfaction of our ambitions: the utmost hopes of riches or power which each one of you cherishes will be far surpassed, and whoever wishes to return home will be allowed to go, either with me or without me. I will make those who stay the envy of those who return.

2

Abraham Lincoln

'Government of the people, by the people, for the people, shall not perish from the earth.'

∿

On 1 June 1865, Senator Charles Sumner referred to the most famous speech given by President Abraham Lincoln. In his eulogy on the slain president, he called the Gettysburg Address a 'monumental act.' He said Lincoln was mistaken that 'the world will little note, nor long remember what we say here.' Rather, the Bostonian remarked, 'The world noted at once what he said, and will never cease to remember it. The battle itself was less important than the speech.'

The Gettysburg Address

Gettysburg, Pennsylvania
19 November 1863

Four score and seven years ago our fathers brought forth on this continent a new nation, conceived in Liberty, and dedicated to the proposition that all men are created equal.

Now we are engaged in a great civil war, testing whether that nation, or any nation so conceived and so dedicated, can long endure. We are met on a great battlefield of that war. We have come to dedicate a portion of that field, as a final resting place for those who here gave their lives that that nation might live. It is altogether fitting and proper that we should do this.

But, in a larger sense, we cannot dedicate—we cannot consecrate, we cannot hallow—this ground.

The brave men, living and dead, who struggled here, have consecrated it, far above our poor power to add or detract. The world will little note, nor long remember what we say here, but it can never forget what they did here. It is for us, the living, rather, to be dedicated here to the unfinished work which they who fought here have thus far so nobly advanced. It is rather for us to be here dedicated to the great task remaining before us—that from these honoured dead we take increased devotion to that cause for which they gave the last full measure of devotion—that we here highly resolve that these dead shall not have died in vain—that this nation, under God, shall have a new birth of freedom—and that government of the people, by the people, for the people, shall not perish from the earth.

SPEECHES TO OHIO REGIMENTS

During the summer of 1864 when President Abraham Lincoln was deeply discouraged about the outcome of the war and his chances for re-election, he asked some Ohio soldiers to stop at the White House before returning home. The two speeches which follow express more than his appreciation—they reveal his vision of democracy and hope for the future.

Speech to the One Hundred Sixty-fourth Ohio Regiment

Washington, D.C.
18 August 1864

Soldiers, you are about to return to your homes and your friends, after having, as I learn, performed in camp a comparatively short term of duty in this great contest. I am greatly obliged to you, and to all who have come forward at the call of their country. I wish it might be more generally and universally understood what the country is now engaged in. We have, as all will agree, a free government, where every man has a right to be equal with every other man. In this great struggle, this form of government and every form of human right is endangered if our enemies succeed. There is more involved in this contest than is realized by everyone. There is involved in this struggle the question whether your children and my children shall enjoy the privileges we have enjoyed. I say this in order to impress upon you, if you are not already so impressed, that no small matter should divert us from our great purpose. There may be some irregularities in the practical application of our system. It is fair that each man shall pay taxes in exact proportion to the value of his property; but if we should wait before collecting a tax to adjust the taxes upon each man in exact proportion with every other man, we should never collect any tax at all. There may be mistakes made sometimes; things may be done wrong while the officers of the government do all they can to prevent mistakes. But I beg of you, as citizens of this great Republic, not to let your minds be carried off from the great work we have before us. This struggle is too large for you to be diverted from it by any small matter. When you return to your homes rise up to the height of a generation of men worthy of a free government, and we will carry out the great work we have commenced. I return to you my sincere thanks, soldiers, for the honour you have done me this afternoon.

◆

This speech of Lincoln shows his admiration for the common soldier.

Speech to the One Hundred Sixty-sixth Ohio Regiment

Washington, D.C.
22 August 1864

I suppose you are going home to see your families and friends. For the service you have done in this great struggle in which we are engaged, I present you sincere thanks for myself and the country. I almost always feel inclined, when I happen to say anything to soldiers, to impress upon them in a few brief remarks the importance of success in this contest. It is not merely for today, but for all time to come that we should perpetuate for our children's children this great and free government, which we have enjoyed all our lives. I beg you to remember this, not merely for my sake, but for yours. I happen temporarily to occupy this big White House. I am a living witness that any one of your children may look to come here as my father's child has. It is in order that each of you may have through this free government which we have enjoyed, an open field and a fair chance for your industry, enterprise and intelligence; that you may all have equal privileges in the race of life, with all its desirable human aspirations. It is for this the struggle should be maintained, that we may not lose our birthright—not only for one, but for two or three years. The nation is worth fighting for, to secure such an inestimable jewel.

◆

Two days after the surrender of Confederate General Robert E. Lee virtually ended the Civil War, a jubilant crowd gathered outside the White House, calling for President Lincoln. Reporter Noah Brooks wrote, 'Outside was a vast sea of faces, illuminated by the lights that burned in the festal array of the White House, and stretching far out into the misty darkness. It was a silent, intent, and perhaps surprised, multitude. Within stood the tall, gaunt figure of the President, deeply thoughtful, intent upon the elucidation of the generous policy which should be pursued toward the South. That this was not the sort of speech which the multitude had expected is tolerably certain.' Lincoln stood at the window over the building's main north door, a place where presidents customarily gave speeches. Brooks held a light so Lincoln could read his speech, while young Tad Lincoln grasped the pages as they fluttered to his feet. The speech introduced the complex topic of reconstruction, especially as it related to the state of Louisiana. For the first time in a public setting, Lincoln expressed his support for black suffrage. This statement incensed John Wilkes Booth, a member of the audience, who vowed, 'That is the last speech he will make.' A white supremacist and Confederate activist, Booth made good on his threat three days later.

Last Public Address

White House, Washington D.C.
11 April 1865

We meet this evening, not in sorrow, but in gladness of heart. The evacuation of Petersburg and Richmond, and the surrender of the principal insurgent army, give hope of a righteous and speedy peace whose joyous expression cannot be restrained. In the midst of this, however, He from whom all blessings flow, must not be forgotten. A call for a national thanksgiving is being prepared, and will be duly promulgated. Nor must those whose harder part gives us the cause of rejoicing, be overlooked. Their honours must not be parcelled out with others. I myself was near the front, and had the high pleasure of transmitting much of the good news to you; but no part of the honour, for plan or execution, is mine. To General Grant, his skilful officers, and brave men, all belongs. The gallant Navy stood ready, but was not in reach to take active part.

By these recent successes the reinauguration of the national authority—reconstruction—which has had a large share of thought from the first, is pressed much more closely upon our attention. It is fraught with great difficulty. Unlike a case of a war between independent nations, there is no authorized organ for us to treat with. No one man has authority to give up the rebellion for any other man. We simply must begin with, and mould from, disorganized and discordant elements. Nor is it a small additional embarrassment that we, the loyal people, differ among ourselves as to the mode, manner and means of reconstruction.

As a general rule, I abstain from reading the reports of attacks upon myself, wishing not to be provoked by that to which I cannot properly offer an answer. In spite of this precaution, however, it comes to my knowledge that I am much censured for some supposed agency in setting up, and seeking to sustain, the new state government of Louisiana. In this I have done just so much as, and no more than, the public knows. In the Annual Message of December 1863 and accompanying Proclamation, I presented a plan of reconstruction (as the phrase goes) which, I promised, if adopted by any State, should be acceptable to, and sustained by, the Executive government of the nation. I distinctly stated that this was not the only plan which might possibly be acceptable; and I also distinctly protested that the Executive claimed no right to say when, or whether members should be admitted to seats in Congress from such States. This plan was, in advance, submitted to the then Cabinet, and distinctly approved by every member of it. One of them suggested that I should then, and in that connection, apply the Emancipation Proclamation to the theretofore excepted parts of Virginia and Louisiana; that I should drop the suggestion about apprenticeship for freed people, and that I should omit the protest against my own power, in regard to the admission of members to Congress; but even he approved every part and parcel of the plan which has since been employed or touched by the action of Louisiana. The new constitution of Louisiana, declaring emancipation for the whole State, practically applies the Proclamation to the part previously accepted. It does not adopt apprenticeship for freed people; and it is silent, as it could not well be otherwise, about the admission of members to Congress. So that, as it applies to Louisiana, every member of the Cabinet fully approved the plan. The message went to Congress, and I received many commendations of the plan, written and verbal; and not a single objection to it, from any professed emancipationist, came to my knowledge, until after the news reached Washington that the people of Louisiana had begun to move in accordance with it. From about July 1862, I had corresponded with different persons, supposed to be interested, seeking a reconstruction of a state government for Louisiana. When the message of 1863, with the plan before mentioned, reached New Orleans, General Banks wrote me that he was confident the people, with his military cooperation, would reconstruct, substantially on that plan. I wrote him, and some of them to try it; they tried it, and the result is known. Such only has been my agency in getting up the Louisiana government. As to sustaining it, my promise is out, as before stated. But, as bad promises are better broken than kept, I shall treat this as a bad promise, and break it, whenever I shall be convinced that keeping it is adverse to the public interest. But I have not yet been so convinced.

I have been shown a letter on this subject, supposed to be an able one, in which the writer expresses regret that my mind has not seemed to be definitely fixed on the question whether the seceding States, so called, are in the Union or out of it. It would perhaps add astonishment to his regret, were he to learn that since I have found professed Union men endeavouring to make that question, I have *purposely* forborne any public expression upon it. As appears to me, that question has not been, nor yet is, a practically material one, and that any discussion of it, while it thus remains practically immaterial, could have no effect other than the mischievous one of dividing our friends. As yet, whatever it may hereafter become, that question is bad, as the basis of a controversy, and good for nothing at all—a merely pernicious abstraction.

We all agree that the seceded States, so called, are out of their proper relation with the Union; and that the sole object of the government, civil and military, in regard to those States is to again get them into that proper practical relation. I believe it is not only possible, but in fact, easier to do this, without deciding, or even considering, whether these States have ever been out of the Union, than with it. Finding themselves safely at home, it would be utterly immaterial whether they had ever been abroad. Let us all join in doing the acts necessary to restoring the proper practical relations between these States and the Union; and each forever after, innocently indulge his own opinion whether, in doing the acts, he brought the States from without, into the Union, or only gave them proper assistance, they never having been out of it.

The amount of constituency, so to speak, on which the new Louisiana government rests, would be more satisfactory to all, if it contained fifty, thirty, or even twenty thousand, instead of only about twelve thousand, as it does. It is also unsatisfactory to some that the elective franchise is not given to the coloured man. I would myself prefer that it were now conferred on the very intelligent, and on those who serve our cause as soldiers. Still the question is not whether the Louisiana government, as it stands, is quite all that is desirable. The question is, 'Will it be wiser to take it as it is, and help to improve it; or to reject, and disperse it? Can Louisiana be brought into proper practical relation with the Union sooner by sustaining, or by discarding her new state government?' Some twelve thousand voters in the heretofore slave-state of Louisiana have sworn allegiance to the Union, assumed to be the rightful political power of the state, held elections, organized a state government, adopted a free-state constitution, giving the benefit of public schools equally to black and white, and empowering the Legislature to confer the elective franchise upon the coloured man. Their Legislature has already voted to ratify the constitutional amendment recently passed by Congress, abolishing slavery throughout the nation. These twelve thousand persons are thus fully committed to the Union, and to perpetual freedom in the state—committed to the very things, and nearly all the things the nation wants—and they ask the nation's recognition and its assistance to make good their committal. Now, if we reject and spurn them, we do our utmost to disorganize and disperse them. We in effect say to the white men, 'You are worthless, or worse—we will neither help you, nor be helped by you.' To the blacks we say, 'This cup of liberty which these, your old masters, hold to your lips, we will dash from you, and leave you to the chances of gathering the spilled and scattered contents in some vague and undefined when, where and how.' If this course, discouraging and paralyzing both white and black, has any tendency to bring Louisiana into proper practical relations with the Union, I have, so far, been unable to perceive it. If, on the contrary, we recognize and sustain the new government of Louisiana the converse of all this is made true. We encourage the hearts, and nerve the arms of the twelve thousand to adhere to their work, and argue for it, and proselyte for it, and fight for it, and feed it, and grow it, and ripen it to a complete success. The coloured man too, in seeing all united for him, is inspired with vigilance, and energy, and daring, to the same end. Grant that he desires the elective franchise, will he not attain it sooner by saving the already advanced steps toward it, than by running backward over them? Concede that the new government of Louisiana is only to what it should be as the egg is to the fowl, we shall sooner have the fowl by hatching the egg than by smashing it? Again, if we reject Louisiana, we also reject one vote in favour of the proposed amendment to the national Constitution. To meet this proposition, it has been argued that no more than three-fourths of those states which have not attempted secession are necessary to validly ratify the amendment. I do not commit myself against this, further than to say that such a ratification would be questionable, and sure to be persistently questioned; while a ratification by three-fourths of all the states would be unquestioned and unquestionable.

I repeat the question, 'Can Louisiana be brought into proper practical relation with the Union *sooner* by *sustaining* or by *discarding* her new state government?'

What has been said of Louisiana will apply generally to other states. And yet so great peculiarities pertain to each state, and such important and sudden changes occur in the same state; and withal, so new and unprecedented is the whole case, that no exclusive, and inflexible plan can be safely prescribed as to details and collaterals. Such an exclusive, and inflexible plan, would surely become a new entanglement. Important principles may, and must, be inflexible.

In the present *'situation'* as the phrase goes, it may be my duty to make some new announcement to the people of the South. I am considering, and shall not fail to act, when satisfied that action will be proper.

3

Che Guevara

'We want peace. We want to build a better life for our people. That is why we avoid, insofar as possible, falling into the provocations manufactured by the Yankees.'

∿

On 11 December 1964, Guevara gave an inflammatory speech at the United Nations General Assembly, wherein he vehemently attacked the west and specifically the United States of America. It created quite a news that day. Several member states were up against Che Guevara and they took to the floor to challenge him.

Speech at the United Nations

General Assembly of the United Nations, New York
11 December 1964

Mr President, distinguished delegates, the delegation of

Cuba to this Assembly, first of all, is pleased to fulfil the agreeable duty of welcoming the addition of three new nations to the important number of those that discuss the problems of the world here. We therefore greet, in the persons of their presidents and prime ministers, the people of Zambia, Malawi and Malta, and express the hope that from the outset these countries will be added to the group of non-aligned countries that struggle against imperialism, colonialism and neo-colonialism.

We also wish to convey our congratulations to the president of this Assembly (Alex Quaison-Sackey of Ghana), whose elevation to so high a post is of special significance since it reflects this new historic stage of resounding triumphs for the people of Africa, who up until recently were subject to the colonial system of imperialism. Today, in their immense majority, these people have become sovereign states through the legitimate exercise of their self-determination. The final hour of colonialism has struck, and millions of inhabitants of Africa, Asia and Latin America rise to meet a new life and demand their unrestricted right to self-determination and to the independent development of their nations.

We wish you, Mr President, the greatest success in the tasks entrusted to you by the member states.

Cuba comes here to state its position on the most important points of controversy and will do so with the full sense of responsibility that the use of this rostrum implies, while at the same time fulfilling the unavoidable duty of speaking clearly and frankly.

We would like to see this Assembly shake itself out of complacency and move forward. We would like to see the committees begin their work and not stop at the first confrontation. Imperialism wants to turn this meeting into a pointless oratorical tournament, instead of solving the serious problems of the world. We must prevent it from doing so. This session of the Assembly should not be remembered in the future solely by the Number 19 that identifies it. Our efforts are directed to that end.

We feel that we have the right and the obligation to do so, because our country is one of the most constant points of friction. It is one of the places where the principles upholding the right of small countries to sovereignty are put to the test day by day, minute by minute. At the same time our country is one of the trenches of freedom in the world, situated a few steps away from U.S. imperialism, showing by its actions, its daily example, that in the present conditions of humanity the people can liberate themselves and can keep themselves free.

Of course, there now exists a socialist camp that becomes stronger day by day and has more powerful weapons of struggle. But additional conditions are required for survival: the maintenance of internal unity, faith in one's own destiny, and the irrevocable decision to fight to the death for the defence of one's country and revolution. These conditions, distinguished delegates, exist in Cuba.

Of all the burning problems to be dealt with by this Assembly, one of special significance for us, and one whose solution we feel must be found first—so as to leave no doubt in the minds of anyone—is that of peaceful coexistence among states with different economic and social systems. Much progress has been made in the world in this field. But imperialism, particularly U.S. imperialism, has attempted to make the world believe that peaceful coexistence is the exclusive right of the earth's great powers. We say here what our president said in Cairo, and what later was expressed in the declaration of the Second Conference of Heads of State or Government of Nonaligned Countries: that peaceful coexistence cannot be limited to the powerful countries if we want to ensure world peace. Peaceful coexistence must be exercised among all states, regardless of size, regardless of the previous historical relations that linked them, and regardless of the problems that may arise among some of them at a given moment.

At present, the type of peaceful coexistence to which we aspire is often violated. Merely because the Kingdom of Cambodia maintained a neutral attitude and did not bow to the machinations of U.S. imperialism, it has been subjected to all kinds of treacherous and brutal attacks from the Yankee bases in South Vietnam.

Laos, a divided country, has also been the object of imperialist aggression of every kind. Its people have been massacred from the air. The conventions concluded at Geneva have been violated, and part of its territory is in constant danger of cowardly attacks by imperialist forces.

The Democratic Republic of Vietnam knows all these

histories of aggression as do few nations on earth. It has once again seen its frontier violated, has seen enemy bombers and fighter planes attack its installations, and U.S. warships, violating territorial waters, attack its naval posts. At this time, the threat hangs over the Democratic Republic of Vietnam that the U.S. war makers may openly extend into its territory the war that for many years they have been waging against the people of South Vietnam. The Soviet Union and the People's Republic of China have given serious warnings to the United States. We are faced with a case in which world peace is in danger and, moreover, the lives of millions of human beings in this part of Asia are constantly threatened and subjected to the whim of the U.S. invader.

Peaceful coexistence has also been brutally put to the test in Cyprus, due to pressures from the Turkish government and NATO, compelling the people and the government of Cyprus to make a heroic and firm stand in defence of their sovereignty.

In all these parts of the world, imperialism attempts to impose its version of what coexistence should be. It is the oppressed people in alliance with the socialist camp that must show them what true coexistence is, and it is the obligation of the United Nations to support them.

We must also state that it is not only in relations among sovereign states that the concept of peaceful coexistence needs to be precisely defined. As Marxists we have maintained that peaceful coexistence among nations does not encompass coexistence between the exploiters and the exploited, between the oppressors and the oppressed. Furthermore, the right to full independence from all forms of colonial oppression is a fundamental principle of this organization. That is why we express our solidarity with the colonial people of so-called Portuguese Guinea, Angola and Mozambique, who have been massacred for the crime of demanding their freedom. And we are prepared to help them to the extent of our ability in accordance with the Cairo declaration.

We express our solidarity with the people of Puerto Rico and their great leader, Pedro Albizu Campos, who, in another act of hypocrisy, has been set free at the age of 72, almost unable to speak, paralyzed, after spending a lifetime in jail. Albizu Campos is a symbol of the as yet unfree but indomitable Latin America. Years and years of prison, almost unbearable pressures in jail, mental torture, solitude, total isolation from his people and his family, the insolence of the conqueror and its lackeys in the land of his birth— nothing broke his will. The delegation of Cuba, on behalf of its people, pays a tribute of admiration and gratitude to a patriot who confers honour upon our America.

The United States for many years has tried to convert Puerto Rico into a model of hybrid culture: the Spanish language with English inflexions, the Spanish language with hinges on its backbone—the better to bow down before the Yankee soldier. Puerto Rican soldiers have been used as cannon fodder in imperialist wars, as in Korea, and have even been made to fire at their own brothers, as in the massacre perpetrated by the U.S. Army a few months ago against the unarmed people of Panama—one of the most recent crimes carried out by Yankee imperialism. And yet, despite this assault on their will and their historical destiny, the people of Puerto Rico have preserved their culture, their Latin character, their national feelings, which in themselves give proof of the implacable desire for independence lying within the masses on that Latin American island. We must also warn that the principle of peaceful coexistence does not encompass the right to mock the will of the people, as is happening in the case of so-called British Guiana. There the government of Prime Minister Cheddi Jagan has been the victim of every kind of pressure and manoeuvre, and independence has been delayed to gain time to find ways to flout the people's will and guarantee the docility of a new government, placed in power by covert means, in order to grant a castrated freedom to this country of the Americas. Whatever roads Guiana may be compelled to follow to obtain independence, the moral and militant support of Cuba goes to its people.

Furthermore, we must point out that the islands of Guadeloupe and Martinique have been fighting for a long time for self-government without obtaining it. This state of affairs must not continue. Once again we speak out to put the world on guard against what is happening in South Africa. The brutal policy of apartheid is applied before the eyes of the nations of the world. The people of Africa are compelled to endure the fact that on the African continent the superiority of one race over another remains official policy, and that in the name of this racial superiority murder is committed with impunity. Can the United Nations do nothing to stop this?

I would like to refer specifically to the painful case of the Congo, unique in the history of the modern world, which shows how, with absolute impunity, with the most insolent cynicism, the rights of people can be flouted. The direct reason for all this is the enormous wealth of the Congo, which the imperialist countries want to keep under their control. In the speech he made during his first visit to the United Nations, compañero Fidel Castro observed that the whole problem of coexistence among people boils down to the wrongful appropriation of other people's wealth. He made the following statement: 'End the philosophy of plunder and the philosophy of war will be ended as well.' But the philosophy of plunder has not only not been ended, it is stronger than ever. And that is why those who used the name of the United Nations to commit the murder of Lumumba are today, in the name of the defence of the white race, murdering thousands of Congolese. How can we forget the betrayal of the hope that Patrice Lumumba placed in the United Nations? How can we forget the machinations and manoeuvre that followed in the wake of the occupation of that country by UN troops, under whose auspices the assassins of this great African patriot acted with impunity? How can we forget, distinguished delegates, that the one who flouted the authority of the UN in the Congo—and not exactly for patriotic reasons, but rather by virtue of conflicts between imperialists—was Moise Tshombe, who initiated the secession of Katanga with Belgian support? And how can one justify, how can one explain, that at the end of all the United Nations' activities there, Tshombe, dislodged from Katanga, should return as lord and master of the Congo? Who can deny the sad role that the imperialists compelled the United Nations to play?

To sum up: Dramatic mobilizations were carried out to avoid the secession of Katanga, but today Tshombe is in power, the wealth of the Congo is in imperialist hands—and the expenses have to be paid by the honourable nations. The merchants of war certainly do good business! That is why the government of Cuba supports the just stance of the Soviet Union in refusing to pay the expenses for this crime.

And as if this were not enough, we now have flung in our faces these latest acts that have filled the world with indignation. Who are the perpetrators? Belgian paratroopers, carried by U.S. planes, who took off from British bases. We remember as if it were yesterday that we saw a small country in Europe, a civilized and industrious country, the Kingdom of Belgium, invaded by Hitler's hordes. We were embittered by the knowledge that this small nation was massacred by German imperialism, and we felt affection for its people. But this other side of the imperialist coin was the one that many of us did not see. Perhaps the sons of Belgian patriots who died defending their country's liberty are now murdering in cold blood thousands of Congolese in the name of the white race, just as they suffered under the German heel because their blood was not sufficiently Aryan. Our free eyes open now on new horizons and can see what yesterday, in our condition as colonial slaves, we could not observe: that 'Western Civilization' disguises behind its showy facade a picture of hyenas and jackals. That is the only name that can be applied to those who have gone to fulfil such 'humanitarian' tasks in the Congo. A carnivorous animal that feeds on unarmed people. That is what imperialism does to men. That is what distinguishes the imperial 'white man'. All free men of the world must be prepared to avenge the crime of the Congo. Perhaps many of those soldiers, who were turned into subhumans by imperialist machinery, believe in good faith that they are defending the rights of a superior race. In this Assembly, however, those people whose skins are darkened by a different sun, coloured by different pigments, constitute the majority. And they fully and clearly understand that the difference between men does not lie in the colour of their skin, but in the forms of ownership of the means of production, in the relations of production. The Cuban delegation extends greetings to the people of Southern Rhodesia and South-west Africa, oppressed by white colonialist minorities; to the people of Basutoland, Bechuanaland, Swaziland, French Somaliland, the Arabs of Palestine, Aden and the Protectorates, Oman; and to all people in conflict with imperialism and colonialism. We reaffirm our support to them.

I express also the hope that there will be a just solution

to the conflict facing our sister republic of Indonesia in its relations with Malaysia. Mr President: one of the fundamental themes of this conference is general and complete disarmament. We express our support for general and complete disarmament. Furthermore, we advocate the complete destruction of all thermonuclear devices and we support the holding of a conference of all the nations of the world to make this aspiration of all people a reality. In his statement before this assembly, our prime minister warned that arms races have always led to war. There are new nuclear powers in the world, and the possibilities of a confrontation are growing. We believe that such a conference is necessary to obtain the total destruction of thermonuclear weapons and, as a first step, the total prohibition of tests. At the same time, we have to establish clearly the duty of all countries to respect the present borders of other states and to refrain from engaging in any aggression, even with conventional weapons.

In adding our voice to that of all the people of the world who ask for general and complete disarmament, the destruction of all nuclear arsenals, the complete halt to the building of new thermonuclear devices and of nuclear tests of any kind, we believe it necessary to also stress that the territorial integrity of nations must be respected and the armed hand of imperialism held back, for it is no less dangerous when it uses only conventional weapons. Those who murdered thousands of defenceless citizens of the Congo did not use the atomic bomb. They used conventional weapons. Conventional weapons have also been used by imperialism, causing so many deaths.

Even if the measures advocated here were to become effective and make it unnecessary to mention it, we must point out that we cannot adhere to any regional pact for denuclearization so long as the United States maintains aggressive bases on our own territory, in Puerto Rico, Panama and in other Latin American states where it feels it has the right to place both conventional and nuclear weapons without any restrictions. We feel that we must be able to provide for our own defence in the light of the recent resolution of the Organization of American States against Cuba, on the basis of which an attack may be carried out invoking the Rio Treaty. If the conference to which we have just referred were to achieve all these objectives—which, unfortunately, would be difficult—we believe it would be the most important one in the history of humanity. To ensure this it would be necessary for the People's Republic of China to be represented, and that is why a conference of this type must be held. But it would be much simpler for the people of the world to recognize the undeniable truth of the existence of the People's Republic of China, whose government is the sole representative of its people, and to give it the seat it deserves, which is, at present, usurped by the gang that controls the province of Taiwan, with U.S. support.

The problem of the representation of China in the United Nations cannot in any way be considered as a case of a new admission to the organization, but rather as the restoration of the legitimate rights of the People's Republic of China.

We must repudiate energetically the 'two Chinas' plot. The Chiang Kai-shek gang of Taiwan cannot remain in the United Nations. What we are dealing with, we repeat, is the expulsion of the usurper and the installation of the legitimate representative of the Chinese people.

We also warn against the U.S. Government's insistence on presenting the problem of the legitimate representation of China in the UN as an 'important question', in order to impose a requirement of a two-thirds majority of members present and voting. The admission of the People's Republic of China to the United Nations is, in fact, an important question for the entire world, but not for the machinery of the United Nations, where it must constitute a mere question of procedure. In this way justice will be done. Almost as important as attaining justice, however, would be the demonstration, once and for all, that this August Assembly has eyes to see, ears to hear, tongues to speak with and sound criteria for making its decisions. The proliferation of nuclear weapons among the member states of NATO, and especially the possession of these devices of mass destruction by the Federal Republic of Germany, would make the possibility of an agreement on disarmament even more remote, and linked to such an agreement is the problem of the peaceful reunification of Germany. So long as there is no clear understanding, the existence of two Germanys must be recognized: that of the German Democratic Republic and the Federal Republic. The German problem can be solved only with the direct participation in negotiations of the German Democratic Republic with full rights. We shall only touch on the questions of economic development and international trade that are broadly represented in the agenda. In this very year of 1964 the Geneva conference was held at which a multitude of matters related to these aspects of international relations were dealt with. The warnings and forecasts of our delegation were fully confirmed, to the misfortune of the economically dependent countries.

We wish only to point out that insofar as Cuba is concerned, the United States of America has not implemented the explicit recommendations of that conference, and recently the U.S. Government also prohibited the sale of medicines to Cuba. By doing so it divested itself, once and for all, of the mask of humanitarianism with which it attempted to disguise the aggressive nature of its blockade against the people of Cuba.

Furthermore, we state once more that the scars left by colonialism that impede the development of the people are expressed not only in political relations. The so-called deterioration of the terms of trade is nothing but the result of the unequal exchange between countries producing raw materials and industrial countries, which dominate markets and impose the illusory justice of equal exchange of values.

So long as the economically dependent people do not free themselves from the capitalist markets and, in a firm bloc with the socialist countries, impose new relations between the exploited and the exploiters, there will be no solid economic development. In certain cases there will be retrogression, in which the weak countries will fall under the political domination of the imperialists and colonialists.

Finally, distinguished delegates, it must be made clear that in the area of the Caribbean, manoeuvres and preparations for aggression against Cuba are taking place, on the coasts of Nicaragua above all, in Costa Rica as well, in the Panama Canal Zone, on Vieques Island in Puerto Rico, in Florida and possibly in other parts of U.S. territory and perhaps also in Honduras. In these places Cuban mercenaries are training, as well as mercenaries of other nationalities, with a purpose that cannot be the most peaceful one. After a big scandal, the government of Costa Rica—it is said—has ordered the elimination of all training camps of Cuban exiles in that country.

No-one knows whether this position is sincere, or whether it is a simple alibi because the mercenaries training there were about to commit some misdeed. We hope that full cognizance will be taken of the real existence of bases for aggression, which we denounced long ago, and that the world will ponder the international responsibility of the government of a country that authorizes and facilitates the training of mercenaries to attack Cuba. We should note that news of the training of mercenaries in different parts in the Caribbean and the participation of the U.S. Government in such acts is presented as completely natural in the newspapers in the United States. We know of no Latin American voice that has officially protested this. This shows the cynicism with which the U.S. Government moves its pawns.

The sharp foreign ministers of the OAS had eyes to see Cuban emblems and to find 'irrefutable' proof in the weapons that the Yankees exhibited in Venezuela, but they do not see the preparations for aggression in the United States, just as they did not hear the voice of President Kennedy, who explicitly declared himself the aggressor against Cuba at Playa Girón [Bay of Pigs invasion of April 1961]. In some cases, it is a blindness provoked by the hatred against our revolution by the ruling classes of the Latin American countries. In others—and these are sadder and more deplorable—it is the product of the dazzling glitter of mammon.

As is well known, after the tremendous commotion of the so-called Caribbean crisis, the United States undertook certain commitments with the Soviet Union. These culminated in the withdrawal of certain types of weapons that the continued acts of aggression of the United States— such as the mercenary attack at Playa Girón and threats of invasion against our homeland—had compelled us to install in Cuba as an act of legitimate and essential defence.

The United States, furthermore, tried to get the UN to inspect our territory. But we emphatically refuse, since Cuba does not recognize the right of the United States, or of anyone else in the world, to determine the type of weapons Cuba may have within its borders.

In this connection, we would abide only by multilateral agreements, with equal obligations for all the parties concerned. As Fidel Castro has said, 'So long as the concept of sovereignty exists as the prerogative of nations and of independent people, as a right of all people, we will not accept the exclusion of our people from that right. So long as the world is governed by these principles, so long as the world is governed by those concepts that have universal validity because they are universally accepted and recognized by the people, we will not accept the attempt to deprive us of any of those rights, and we will renounce none of those rights.' The Secretary-General of the United Nations, U Thant, understood our reasons. Nevertheless, the United States attempted to establish a new prerogative, an arbitrary and illegal one: that of violating the airspace of a small country. Thus, we see flying over our country U-2 aircraft and other types of spy planes that, with complete impunity, fly over our airspace. We have made all the necessary warnings for the violations of our airspace to cease, as well as for a halt to the provocations of the U.S. Navy against our sentry posts in the zone of Guantánamo, the buzzing by aircraft of our ships or the ships of other nationalities in international waters, the pirate attacks against ships sailing under different flags, and the infiltration of spies, saboteurs and weapons onto our island.

We want to build socialism. We have declared that we are supporters of those who strive for peace. We have declared ourselves to be within the group of non-aligned countries, although we are Marxist-Leninists, because the non-aligned countries, like ourselves, fight imperialism. We want peace. We want to build a better life for our people. That is why we avoid, insofar as possible, falling into the provocations manufactured by the Yankees. But we know the mentality of those who govern them. They want to make us pay a very high price for that peace. We reply that the price cannot go beyond the bounds of dignity.

And Cuba reaffirms once again the right to maintain on its territory the weapons it deems appropriate, and its refusal to recognize the right of any power on earth—no matter how powerful—to violate our soil, our territorial waters, or our airspace.

If in any assembly Cuba assumes obligations of a collective nature, it will fulfil them to the letter. So long as this does not happen, Cuba maintains all its rights, just as any other nation. In the face of the demands of imperialism, our prime minister laid out the five points necessary for the existence of a secure peace in the Caribbean. They are:

1. A halt to the economic blockade and all economic and trade pressures by the United States, in all parts of the world, against our country

2. A halt to all subversive activities, launching and landing of weapons and explosives by air and sea, organization of mercenary invasions, infiltration of spies and saboteurs, acts all carried out from the territory of the United States and some accomplice countries

3. A halt to pirate attacks carried out from existing bases in the United States and Puerto Rico
4. A halt to all the violations of our airspace and our territorial waters by U.S. aircraft and warships
5. Withdrawal from the Guantánamo naval base and return of the Cuban territory occupied by the United States

None of these elementary demands has been met, and our forces are still being provoked from the naval base at Guantánamo. That base has become a nest of thieves and a launching pad for them into our territory. We would tire this Assembly were we to give a detailed account of the large number of provocations of all kinds. Suffice it to say that including the first days of December, the number amounts to 1,323 in 1964 alone. The list covers minor provocations such as violation of the boundary line, launching of objects from the territory controlled by the United States, the commission of acts of sexual exhibitionism by U.S. personnel of both sexes, and verbal insults. It includes others that are more serious, such as shooting off small calibre weapons, aiming weapons at our territory, and offenses against our national flag. Extremely serious provocations include those of crossing the boundary line and starting fires in installations on the Cuban side, as well as rifle fire. There have been 78 rifle shots this year, with the sorrowful toll of one death: that of Ramón López Peña, a soldier, killed by two shots fired from the U.S. post three and a half kilometre from the coast on the northern boundary. This extremely grave provocation took place at 7:07 p.m. on 19 July 1964, and the prime minister of our government publicly stated on 26 July that if the event were to recur he would give orders for our troops to repel the aggression. At the same time orders were given for the withdrawal of the forward line of Cuban forces to positions farther away from the boundary line and construction of the necessary fortified positions. One thousand three hundred and twenty-three provocations in 340 days amount to approximately four per day. Only a perfectly disciplined army with a morale such as ours could resist so many hostile acts without losing its self-control.

Forty-seven countries meeting at the Second Conference of Heads of State or Government of Non-aligned Countries in Cairo unanimously agreed.

Noting with concern that foreign military bases are in practice a means of bringing pressure on nations and retarding their emancipation and development, based on their own ideological, political, economic and cultural ideas, the conference declares its unreserved support to the countries that are seeking to secure the elimination of foreign bases from their territory and calls upon all states maintaining troops and bases in other countries to remove them immediately. The conference considers that the maintenance at Guantánamo (Cuba) of a military base of the United States of America, in defiance of the will of the government and people of Cuba and in defiance of the provisions embodied in the declaration of the Belgrade conference, constitutes a violation of Cuba's sovereignty and territorial integrity.

Noting that the Cuban government expresses its readiness to settle its dispute over the base at Guantánamo with the United States of America on an equal footing, the conference urges the U.S. Government to open negotiations with the Cuban government to evacuate their base.

The government of the United States has not responded to this request of the Cairo conference and is attempting to maintain indefinitely by force its occupation of a piece of our territory, from which it carries out acts of aggression such as those detailed earlier.

The Organization of American States—which the people also call the U.S. Ministry of Colonies—condemned us 'energetically', even though it had just excluded us from its midst, ordering its members to break off diplomatic and trade relations with Cuba. The OAS authorized aggression against our country at any time and under any pretext, violating the most fundamental international laws, completely disregarding the United Nations. Uruguay, Bolivia, Chile and Mexico opposed that measure, and the government of the United States of Mexico refused to comply with the sanctions that had been approved. Since then we have had no relations with any Latin American countries except Mexico, and this fulfils one of the necessary conditions for direct aggression by imperialism.

We want to make clear once again that our concern for Latin America is based on the ties that unite us: the language we speak, the culture we maintain, and the common master we had. We have no other reason for desiring the liberation of Latin America from the U.S. colonial yoke. If any of the Latin American countries here decide to re-establish relations with Cuba, we would be willing to do so on the basis of equality, and without viewing that recognition of Cuba as a free country in the world to be a gift to our government. We won that recognition with our blood in the days of the liberation struggle. We acquired it with our blood in the defence of our shores against the Yankee invasion.

Although we reject any accusations against us of interference in the internal affairs of other countries, we cannot deny that we sympathize with those people who strive for their freedom. We must fulfil the obligation of our government and people to state clearly and categorically to the world that we morally support and stand in solidarity with people who struggle anywhere in the world to make a reality of the rights of full sovereignty proclaimed in the UN Charter.

It is the United States that intervenes. It has done so historically in Latin America. Since the end of the last century Cuba has experienced this truth; but it has been experienced, too, by Venezuela, Nicaragua, Central America in general, Mexico, Haiti and the Dominican Republic. In recent years, apart from our people, Panama has experienced direct aggression, where the marines in the Canal Zone opened fire in cold blood against the defenceless people; the Dominican Republic, whose coast was violated by the Yankee fleet to avoid an outbreak of the just fury of the people after the death of Trujillo; and Colombia, whose capital was taken by assault as a result of a rebellion provoked by the assassination of Gaitán. Covert interventions are carried out through military missions that participate in internal repression, organizing forces designed for that purpose in many countries, and also in coups d'état, which have been repeated so frequently on the Latin American continent during recent years. Concretely, U.S. forces intervened in the repression of the people of Venezuela, Colombia and Guatemala, who fought with weapons for their freedom. In Venezuela, not only do U.S. forces advise the army and the police, but they also direct acts of genocide carried out from the air against the peasant population in vast insurgent areas. And the Yankee companies operating there exert pressures of every kind to increase direct interference. The imperialists are preparing to repress the people of the Americas and are establishing an International of Crime.

The United States intervenes in Latin America invoking the defence of free institutions. The time will come when this Assembly will acquire greater maturity and demand of the U.S. Government guarantees for the life of the blacks and Latin Americans who live in that country, most of them U.S. citizens by origin or adoption.

Those who kill their own children and discriminate daily against them because of the colour of their skin, those who let the murderers of blacks remain free, protecting them, and furthermore punishing the black population because they demand their legitimate rights as free men—how can those who do this consider themselves guardians of freedom? We understand that today the Assembly is not in a position to ask for explanations of these acts. It must be clearly established, however, that the government of the United States is not the champion of freedom, but rather the perpetrator of exploitation and oppression against the people of the world and against a large part of its own population.

To the ambiguous language with which some delegates have described the case of Cuba and the OAS, we reply with clear-cut words and we proclaim that the people of Latin America will make those servile, sell-out governments pay for their treason.

Cuba, distinguished delegates, a free and sovereign state with no chains binding it to anyone, with no foreign investments on its territory, with no proconsuls directing its policy, can speak with its head held high in this Assembly and can demonstrate the justice of the phrase by which it has been baptized: 'Free Territory of the Americas'. Our example will bear fruit in the continent, as it is already doing to a certain extent in Guatemala, Colombia and Venezuela.

There is no small enemy nor an insignificant force, because no longer are there isolated people. As the Second Declaration of Havana states:

No nation in Latin America is weak—because each forms part of a family of 200 million brothers, who suffer the same miseries, who harbour the same sentiments, who have the same enemy, who dream about the same better future, and who count upon the solidarity of all honest men and women throughout the world... This epic before us is going to be written by the hungry Indian masses, the peasants without land, the exploited workers. It is going to be written by the progressive masses, the honest and brilliant intellectuals, who so greatly abound in our suffering Latin American lands. Struggles of masses and ideas. An epic that will be carried forward by our people, mistreated and scorned by imperialism; our people, unreckoned with until today, who are now beginning to shake off their slumber. Imperialism considered us a weak and submissive flock; and now it begins to be terrified of that flock; a gigantic flock of 200 million Latin Americans in whom Yankee monopoly capitalism now sees its gravediggers... But now from one end of the continent to the other they are signalling with clarity that the hour has come—the hour of their vindication. Now this anonymous mass, this America of colour, sombre, taciturn America, which all over the continent sings with the same sadness and disillusionment, now this mass is beginning to enter definitively into its own history, is beginning to write it with its own blood, is beginning to suffer and die for it.

Because now in the mountains and fields of America, on its flatlands and in its jungles, in the wilderness or in the traffic of cities, on the banks of its great oceans or rivers, this world is beginning to tremble. Anxious hands are stretched forth, ready to die for what is theirs, to win those rights that were laughed at by one and all for 500 years. Yes, now history will have to take the poor of America into account, the exploited and spurned of America, who have decided to begin writing their history for themselves for all time. Already they can be seen on the roads, on foot, day after day, in endless march of hundreds of kilometres to the governmental 'eminences', there to obtain their rights.

Already they can be seen armed with stones, sticks, machetes, in one direction and another, each day, occupying lands, sinking hooks into the land that belongs to them and defending it with their lives. They can be seen carrying signs, slogans, flags; letting them flap in the mountain or prairie winds. And the wave of anger, of demands for justice, of claims for rights trampled underfoot, which is beginning to sweep the lands of Latin America, will not stop. That wave will swell with every passing day. For that wave is composed of the greatest number, the majorities in every respect, those whose labour amasses the wealth and turns the wheels of history. Now they are awakening from the long, brutalizing sleep to which they had been subjected.

For this great mass of humanity has said, 'Enough!' and has begun to march. And their march of giants will not be halted until they conquer true independence—for which they have vainly died more than once. Today, however, those who die will die like the Cubans at Playa Girón. They will die for their own true and never-to-be-surrendered independence.

All this, distinguished delegates, this new will of a whole continent, of Latin America, is made manifest in the cry proclaimed daily by our masses as the irrefutable expression of their decision to fight and to paralyze the armed hand of the invader. It is a cry that has the understanding and support of all the people of the world and especially of the socialist camp, headed by the Soviet Union.

That cry is: Patria o muerte! [Homeland or death!]

4

Franklin D. Roosevelt

'This Nation is asking for action, and action now.'

∿

Franklin D. Roosevelt became the 32nd U.S. President during the worst crisis America had faced since the Civil War. By early 1933, the U.S. economy had sunk to its lowest point in the period known as the Great Depression. Over 13 million Americans were unemployed while wages had declined 60 per cent in value. People lost their lives' savings, their homes and farms. Some began to lose faith in the American system of democracy itself. In this speech, President Roosevelt first tries to calm the fear gripping Americans, and then outlines some of the 'lines of attack' to be immediately taken in the days and weeks ahead.

First Inaugural Speech

Washington, D.C.
4 March 1933

President Hoover, Mr Chief Justice, my friends, this is a day of national consecration. And I am certain that on this day my fellow Americans expect that on my induction into the Presidency I will address them with a candour and a decision which the present situation of our people impels. This is pre-eminently the time to speak the truth, the whole truth, frankly and boldly. Nor need we shrink from honestly facing conditions in our country today. This great Nation will endure as it has endured, will revive and prosper.

So, first of all, let me assert my firm belief that the only thing we have to fear is fear itself—nameless, unreasoning, unjustified terror which paralyzes needed efforts to convert retreat into advance. In every dark hour of our national life a leadership of frankness and of vigour has met with that understanding and support of the people themselves which is essential to victory. And I am convinced that you will again give that support to leadership in these critical days.

In such a spirit on my part and on yours we face our common difficulties. They concern, thank God, only material things. Values have shrunken to fantastic levels; taxes have risen; our ability to pay has fallen; government of all kinds is faced by serious curtailment of income; the means of exchange are frozen in the currents of trade; the withered leaves of industrial enterprise lie on every side; farmers find no markets for their produce; and the savings of many years in thousands of families are gone.

More important, a host of unemployed citizens face the grim problem of existence, and an equally great number toil with little return. Only a foolish optimist can deny the dark realities of the moment.

And yet our distress comes from no failure of substance. We are stricken by no plague of locusts. Compared with the perils which our forefathers conquered because they believed and were not afraid, we still have much to be thankful for. Nature still offers her bounty and human efforts have multiplied it. Plenty is at our doorstep, but a generous use of it languishes in the very sight of the supply. Primarily this is because the rulers of the exchange of mankind's goods have failed, through their own stubbornness and their own incompetence, have admitted their failure, and abdicated. Practices of the unscrupulous money changers stand indicted in the court of public opinion, rejected by the hearts and minds of men.

True they have tried, but their efforts have been cast in the pattern of an outworn tradition. Faced by failure of credit they have proposed only the lending of more money. Stripped of the lure of profit by which to induce our people to follow their false leadership, they have resorted to exhortations, pleading tearfully for restored confidence. They only know the rules of a generation of self-seekers. They have no vision, and when there is no vision the people perish.

Yes, the money changers have fled from their high seats in the temple of our civilization. We may now restore that temple to the ancient truths. The measure of the restoration lies in the extent to which we apply social values more noble than mere monetary profit.

Happiness lies not in the mere possession of money; it lies in the joy of achievement, in the thrill of creative effort. The joy and the moral stimulation of work no longer must be forgotten in the mad chase of evanescent profits. These dark days, my friends, will be worth all they cost us if they teach us that our true destiny is not to be ministered unto but to minister to ourselves and to our fellow men.

Recognition of the falsity of material wealth as the standard of success goes hand in hand with the abandonment of the false belief that public office and high political position are to be valued only by the standards of pride of place and personal profit; and there must be an end to a conduct in banking and in business which too often has given to a sacred trust the likeness of callous and selfish wrongdoing. Small wonder that confidence languishes, for it thrives only on honesty, on honour, on the sacredness of obligations, on faithful protection, and on unselfish performance; without them it cannot live.

Restoration calls, however, not for changes in ethics alone. This Nation is asking for action, and action now.

Our greatest primary task is to put people to work. This is no unsolvable problem if we face it wisely and courageously. It can be accomplished in part by direct recruiting by the government itself, treating the task as we would treat the emergency of a war, but at the same time, through this employment, accomplishing greatly needed projects to stimulate and reorganize the use of our great natural resources.

Hand in hand with that we must frankly recognize the overbalance of population in our industrial centres and, by engaging on a national scale in a redistribution, endeavour to provide a better use of the land for those best fitted for the land. Yes, the task can be helped by definite efforts to raise the values of agricultural products and with this the power to purchase the output of our cities. It can be helped by preventing realistically the tragedy of the growing loss through foreclosure of our small homes and our farms. It can be helped by insistence that the Federal, the State, and the local governments act forthwith on the demand that their cost be drastically reduced. It can be helped by the unifying of relief activities which today are often scattered, uneconomical, unequal. It can be helped by national planning for and supervision of all forms of transportation and of communications and other utilities that have a definitely public character. There are many ways in which it can be helped, but it can never be helped by merely talking about it. We must act. We must act quickly.

And finally, in our progress towards a resumption of work, we require two safeguards against a return of the evils of the old order; there must be a strict supervision of all banking and credits and investments; there must be an end to speculation with other people's money, and there must be provision for an adequate but sound currency.

These, my friends, are the lines of attack. I shall presently urge upon a new Congress in special session detailed measures for their fulfilment, and I shall seek the immediate assistance of the 48 states.

Through this programme of action we address ourselves to putting our own national house in order and making income balance outgo. Our international trade relations, though vastly important, are in point of time and necessity secondary to the establishment of a sound national economy. I favour as a practical policy the putting of first things first. I shall spare no effort to restore world trade by international economic readjustment, but the emergency at home cannot wait on that accomplishment.

The basic thought that guides these specific means of national recovery is not narrowly nationalistic. It is the insistence, as a first consideration, upon the interdependence of the various elements in all parts of the United States of America—a recognition of the old and permanently important manifestation of the American spirit of the pioneer. It is the way to recovery. It is the immediate way. It is the strongest assurance that recovery will endure.

In the field of world policy I would dedicate this Nation to the policy of the good neighbour—the neighbour who resolutely respects himself and, because he does so, respects the rights of others—the neighbour who respects his obligations and respects the sanctity of his agreements in and with a world of neighbours.

If I read the temper of our people correctly, we now realize as we have never realized before our interdependence on each other; that we cannot merely take but we must give as well; that if we are to go forward, we must move as a trained and loyal army willing to sacrifice for the good of a common discipline, because without such discipline no progress can be made, no leadership becomes effective. We are, I know, ready and willing to submit our lives and our property to such discipline, because it makes possible a leadership which aims at the larger good. This I propose to offer, pledging that the larger purposes will bind upon us, bind upon us all as a sacred obligation with a unity of duty hitherto evoked only in times of armed strife.

With this pledge taken, I assume unhesitatingly the leadership of this great army of our people dedicated to a disciplined attack upon our common problems.

Action in this image, action to this end is feasible under the form of government which we have inherited from our ancestors. Our Constitution is so simple, so practical that it is possible always to meet extraordinary needs by changes in emphasis and arrangement without loss of essential form. That is why our constitutional system has proved itself the most superbly enduring political mechanism the modern world has ever seen. It has met every stress of vast expansion of territory, of foreign wars, of bitter internal strife, of world relations.

And it is to be hoped that the normal balance of executive and legislative authority may be wholly adequate to meet the unprecedented task before us. But it may be that an unprecedented demand and need for undelayed action may call for temporary departure from that normal balance of public procedure.

I am prepared under my constitutional duty to recommend the measures that a stricken nation in the midst of a stricken world may require. These measures, or such other measures as the Congress may build out of its experience and wisdom, I shall seek, within my constitutional authority, to bring to speedy adoption.

But in the event that the Congress shall fail to take one of these two courses, in the event that the national emergency is still critical, I shall not evade the clear course of duty that will then confront me. I shall ask the Congress for the one remaining instrument to meet the crisis—broad executive power to wage a war against the emergency, as great as the power that would be given to me if we were in fact invaded by a foreign foe.

For the trust reposed in me, I will return the courage and the devotion that befit the time. I can do no less.

We face the arduous days that lie before us in the warm courage of national unity; with the clear consciousness of seeking old and precious moral values; with the clean satisfaction that comes from the stern performance of duty by the old and young alike. We aim at the assurance of a rounded, permanent national life.

We do not distrust the future of essential democracy. The people of the United States have not failed. In their need they have registered a mandate that they want direct, vigorous action. They have asked for discipline and direction under leadership. They have made me the present instrument of their wishes. In the spirit of the gift I take it.

In this dedication of a Nation we humbly ask the blessing of God. May He protect each and every one of us. May He guide me in the days to come.

◆

The Infamy Speech was a speech delivered by United States President Franklin D. Roosevelt to a Joint Session of the U.S. Congress on 8 December 1941, one day after the Empire of Japan's attack on the U.S. naval base at Pearl Harbor, Hawaii, and the Japanese declaration of war on the United States and the British Empire.

Pearl Harbour Address to the Nation

Washington, D.C.
8 December 1941

Mr Vice President, Mr Speaker, Members of the Senate, and of the House of Representatives, Yesterday, 7 December 1941—a date which will live in infamy—the United States of America was suddenly and deliberately attacked by naval and air forces of the Empire of Japan.

The United States was at peace with that nation and, at the solicitation of Japan, was still in conversation with its government and its emperor looking towards the maintenance of peace in the Pacific.

Indeed, one hour after Japanese air squadrons had commenced bombing in the American island of Oahu, the Japanese ambassador to the United States and his colleague delivered to our Secretary of State a formal reply to a recent American message. And while this reply stated that it seemed useless to continue the existing diplomatic negotiations, it contained no threat or hint of war or of armed attack.

It will be recorded that the distance of Hawaii from Japan makes it obvious that the attack was deliberately planned many days or even weeks ago. During the intervening time, the Japanese government has deliberately sought to deceive the United States by false statements and expressions of hope for continued peace.

The attack yesterday on the Hawaiian islands has caused severe damage to American naval and military forces. I regret to tell you that very many American lives have been lost. In addition, American ships have been reported torpedoed on the high seas between San Francisco and Honolulu.

Yesterday, the Japanese government also launched an attack against Malaya.

Last night, Japanese forces attacked Hong Kong.

Last night, Japanese forces attacked Guam.

Last night, Japanese forces attacked the Philippine Islands.

Last night, the Japanese attacked Wake Island.

And this morning, the Japanese attacked Midway Island.

Japan has, therefore, undertaken a surprise offensive extending throughout the Pacific area. The facts of yesterday and today speak for themselves. The people of the United States have already formed their opinions and well understand the implications to the very life and safety of our nation.

As Commander in Chief of the Army and Navy, I have directed that all measures be taken for our defence. But always will our whole nation remember the character of the onslaught against us.

No matter how long it may take us to overcome this premeditated invasion, the American people in their righteous might will win through to absolute victory.

I believe that I interpret the will of the Congress and of the people when I assert that we will not only defend ourselves to the uttermost, but will also make it very certain that this form of treachery shall never again endanger us.

Hostilities exist. There is no blinking at the fact that our people, our territory, and our interests are in grave danger.

With confidence in our armed forces, with the unbounding determination of our people, we will gain the inevitable triumph—so help us God.

I ask that the Congress declare that since the unprovoked and dastardly attack by Japan on Sunday, 7 December 1941, a state of war has existed between the United States and the Japanese empire.

5

George Washington

'*You will defeat the insidious designs of our enemies, who are compelled to resort from open force to secret artifice.*'

ꞏ

It was the end of the Revolutionary War in America, and an equally terrifying moment was about to happen in the already fledgling American republic. The officers of the Continental Army met in Newburgh, New York. They were discontent with the state of affairs in the army and were seeking a possible insurrection against Congress. Their anger against the Congress was directed at its failure to fulfil the government's promise of decent salary, bounties and life pensions to the army personnel. General Washington personally addressed his grieving men.

Speech Preventing the Revolt of his Officers

New Windsor Cantonment, New York
15 March 1783

Gentlemen, by an anonymous summons, an attempt has been made to convene you together; how inconsistent with the rules of propriety, how unmilitary, and how subversive of all order and discipline, let the good sense of the army decide... Thus much, gentlemen, I have thought it incumbent on me to observe to you, to show upon what principles I opposed the irregular and hasty meeting which was proposed to have been held on Tuesday last—and not because I wanted a disposition to give you every opportunity consistent with your own honour, and the dignity of the army, to make known your grievances. If my conduct heretofore has not evinced to you that I have been a faithful friend to the army, my declaration of it at this time would be equally unavailing and improper. But I was among the first who embarked in the cause of our common country. As I have never left your side one moment, but when called from you on public duty. As I have been the constant companion and witness of your distresses, and not among the last to feel and acknowledge your merits. As I have ever considered my own military reputation as inseparably connected with that of the army. As my heart has ever expanded with joy, when I have heard its praises, and my indignation has arisen, when the mouth of detraction has been opened against it, it can scarcely be supposed, at this late stage of the war, that I am indifferent to its interests.

But how are they to be promoted? The way is plain, says the anonymous addresser. If war continues, remove into the unsettled country, there establish yourselves, and leave an ungrateful country to defend itself. But who are they to defend? Our wives, our children, our farms, and other property which we leave behind us. Or, in this state of hostile separation, are we to take the two first (the latter cannot be removed) to perish in a wilderness, with hunger, cold, and nakedness? If peace takes place, never sheathe your swords, says he, until you have obtained full and ample justice; this dreadful alternative, of either deserting our country in the extremest hour of her distress or turning our arms against it (which is the apparent object, unless Congress can be compelled into instant compliance), has something so shocking in it that humanity revolts at the idea. My God! What can this writer have in view, by recommending such measures? Can he be a friend to the army? Can he be a friend to this country? Rather, is he not an insidious foe? Some emissary, perhaps, from New York, plotting the ruin of both, by sowing the seeds of discord and separation between the civil and military powers of the continent? And what a compliment does he pay to our understandings when he recommends measures in either alternative, impracticable in their nature?

I cannot, in justice to my own belief, and what I have

great reason to conceive is the intention of Congress, conclude this address, without giving it as my decided opinion, that that honourable body entertain exalted sentiments of the services of the army; and, from a full conviction of its merits and sufferings, will do it complete justice. That their endeavours to discover and establish funds for this purpose have been unwearied, and will not cease till they have succeeded, I have not a doubt. But, like all other large bodies, where there is a variety of different interests to reconcile, their deliberations are slow. Why, then, should we distrust them? And, in consequence of that distrust, adopt measures which may cast a shade over that glory which has been so justly acquired; and tarnish the reputation of an army which is celebrated through all Europe, for its fortitude and patriotism? And for what is this done? To bring the object we seek nearer? No! Most certainly, in my opinion, it will cast it at a greater distance.

For myself (and I take no merit in giving the assurance, being induced to it from principles of gratitude, veracity and justice), a grateful sense of the confidence you have ever placed in me, a recollection of the cheerful assistance and prompt obedience I have experienced from you, under every vicissitude of fortune, and the sincere affection I feel for an army I have so long had the honour to command will oblige me to declare, in this public and solemn manner, that, in the attainment of complete justice for all your toils and dangers, and in the gratification of every wish, so far as may be done consistently with the great duty I owe my country and those powers we are bound to respect, you may freely command my services to the utmost of my abilities.

While I give you these assurances, and pledge myself in the most unequivocal manner to exert whatever ability I am possessed of in your favour, let me entreat you, gentlemen, on your part, not to take any measures which, viewed in the calm light of reason, will lessen the dignity and sully the glory you have hitherto maintained; let me request you to rely on the plighted faith of your country, and place a full confidence in the purity of the intentions of Congress; that, previous to your dissolution as an army, they will cause all your accounts to be fairly liquidated, as directed in their resolutions, which were published to you two days ago, and that they will adopt the most effectual measures in their power to render ample justice to you, for your faithful and meritorious services. And let me conjure you, in the name of our common country, as you value your own sacred honour, as you respect the rights of humanity, and as you regard the military and national character of America, to express your utmost horror and detestation of the man who wishes, under any specious pretences, to overturn the liberties of our country, and who wickedly attempts to open the floodgates of civil discord and deluge our rising empire in blood.

By thus determining and thus acting, you will pursue the plain and direct road to the attainment of your wishes. You will defeat the insidious designs of our enemies, who are compelled to resort from open force to secret artifice. You will give one more distinguished proof of unexampled patriotism and patient virtue, rising superior to the pressure of the most complicated sufferings. And you will, by the dignity of your conduct, afford occasion for posterity to say, when speaking of the glorious example you have exhibited to mankind, 'Had this day been wanting, the world had never seen the last stage of perfection to which human nature is capable of attaining.'

6

John F. Kennedy

*'My fellow Americans: ask not what your country can do
for you—ask what you can do for your country.'*

∿

*In a relatively brief address that he spent two months
crafting, Kennedy—at 43, the youngest president elected
to the office and the first Roman Catholic—stressed the
importance of national service.*

Inaugural Address

United States Capitol, Washington, D.C
20 January 1961

Vice President Johnson, Mr Speaker, Mr Chief Justice,
President Eisenhower, Vice President Nixon, President
Truman, reverend clergy, fellow citizens, we observe today

not a victory of party, but a celebration of freedom—symbolizing an end, as well as a beginning—signifying renewal, as well as change. For I have sworn before you and Almighty God the same solemn oath our forebears prescribed nearly a century and three-quarters ago.

The world is very different now. For man holds in his mortal hands the power to abolish all forms of human poverty and all forms of human life. And yet the same revolutionary beliefs for which our forebears fought are still at issue around the globe—the belief that the rights of man come not from the generosity of the state, but from the hand of God.

We dare not forget today that we are the heirs of that first revolution. Let the word go forth from this time and place, to friend and foe alike, that the torch has been passed to a new generation of Americans—born in this century, tempered by war, disciplined by a hard and bitter peace, proud of our ancient heritage, and unwilling to witness or permit the slow undoing of those human rights to which this nation has always been committed, and to which we are committed today at home and around the world.

Let every nation know, whether it wishes us well or ill, that we shall pay any price, bear any burden, meet any hardship, support any friend, oppose any foe, to assure the survival and the success of liberty.

This much we pledge—and more.

To those old allies whose cultural and spiritual origins we share, we pledge the loyalty of faithful friends. United, there is little we cannot do in a host of cooperative ventures. Divided, there is little we can do—for we dare not meet a powerful challenge at odds and split asunder.

To those new states whom we welcome to the ranks of the free, we pledge our word that one form of colonial control shall not have passed away merely to be replaced by a far more iron tyranny. We shall not always expect to find them supporting our view. But we shall always hope to find them strongly supporting their own freedom—and to remember that, in the past, those who foolishly sought power by riding the back of the tiger ended up inside.

To those people in the huts and villages of half the globe struggling to break the bonds of mass misery, we pledge our best efforts to help them help themselves, for whatever period is required—not because the Communists may be doing it, not because we seek their votes, but because it is right. If a free society cannot help the many who are poor, it cannot save the few who are rich.

To our sister republics south of our border, we offer a special pledge: to convert our good words into good deeds, in a new alliance for progress, to assist free men and free governments in casting off the chains of poverty. But this peaceful revolution of hope cannot become the prey of hostile powers. Let all our neighbours know that we shall join with them to oppose aggression or subversion anywhere in the Americas. And let every other power know that this hemisphere intends to remain the master of its own house.

To that world assembly of sovereign states, the United

Nations, our last best hope in an age where the instruments of war have far outpaced the instruments of peace, we renew our pledge of support—to prevent it from becoming merely a forum for invective, to strengthen its shield of the new and the weak, and to enlarge the area in which its writ may run.

Finally, to those nations who would make themselves our adversary, we offer not a pledge but a request: that both sides begin anew the quest for peace, before the dark powers of destruction unleashed by science engulf all humanity in planned or accidental self-destruction.

We dare not tempt them with weakness. For only when our arms are sufficient beyond doubt can we be certain beyond doubt that they will never be employed.

But neither can two great and powerful groups of nations take comfort from our present course—both sides overburdened by the cost of modern weapons, both rightly alarmed by the steady spread of the deadly atom, yet both racing to alter that uncertain balance of terror that stays the hand of mankind's final war.

So let us begin anew—remembering on both sides that civility is not a sign of weakness, and sincerity is always subject to proof. Let us never negotiate out of fear, but let us never fear to negotiate.

Let both sides explore what problems unite us instead of belabouring those problems which divide us.

Let both sides, for the first time, formulate serious and precise proposals for the inspection and control of arms, and bring the absolute power to destroy other nations under the absolute control of all nations.

Let both sides seek to invoke the wonders of science instead of its terrors. Together let us explore the stars, conquer the deserts, eradicate disease, tap the ocean depths, and encourage the arts and commerce.

Let both sides unite to heed, in all corners of the earth, the command of Isaiah—to 'undo the heavy burdens, and [to] let the oppressed go free'.

And, if a beachhead of cooperation may push back the jungle of suspicion, let both sides join in creating a new endeavour—not a new balance of power, but a new world of law—where the strong are just, and the weak secure, and the peace preserved.

All this will not be finished in the first one hundred days. Nor will it be finished in the first one thousand days; nor in the life of this Administration; nor even perhaps in our lifetime on this planet. But let us begin.

In your hands, my fellow citizens, more than mine, will rest the final success or failure of our course. Since this country was founded, each generation of Americans has been summoned to give testimony to its national loyalty. The graves of young Americans who answered the call to service surround the globe.

Now the trumpet summons us again—not as a call to bear arms, though arms we need—not as a call to battle, though embattled we are—but a call to bear the burden of a long twilight struggle, year in and year out, 'rejoicing in hope; patient in tribulation', a struggle against the common enemies of man: tyranny, poverty, disease and war itself.

Can we forge against these enemies a grand and global alliance, North and South, East and West, that can assure a more fruitful life for all mankind? Will you join in that historic effort?

In the long history of the world, only a few generations have been granted the role of defending freedom in its hour of maximum danger. I do not shrink from this responsibility—I welcome it. I do not believe that any of us would exchange places with any other people or any other generation. The energy, the faith, the devotion which we bring to this endeavour will light our country and all who serve it. And the glow from that fire can truly light the world.

And so, my fellow Americans, ask not what your country can do for you; ask what you can do for your country.

My fellow citizens of the world, ask not what America will do for you, but what together we can do for the freedom of man.

Finally, whether you are citizens of America or citizens of the world, ask of us here the same high standards of strength and sacrifice which we ask of you. With a good conscience our only sure reward, with history the final judge of our deeds, let us go forth to lead the land we love, asking His blessing and His help, but knowing that here on earth God's work must truly be our own.

7

Martin Luther King

'*We cannot walk alone.*'

∿

In his iconic speech at the Lincoln Memorial in March of 1963 in Washington for Jobs and Freedom, Martin Luther King urged America to 'make real the promises of democracy'. King synthesized portions of his earlier speeches to capture both the necessity for change and the potential for hope in American society.

I Have a Dream

Lincoln Memorial, Washington, D.C.
28 August 1963

I am happy to join with you today in what will go down in history as the greatest demonstration for freedom in the history of our nation.

Five score years ago, a great American, in whose symbolic shadow we stand today, signed the Emancipation Proclamation. This momentous decree came as a great beacon of light of hope to millions of Negro slaves who had been seared in the flames of withering injustice. It came as a joyous daybreak to end the long night of their captivity.

But one hundred years later, the Negro still is not free. One hundred years later, the life of the Negro is still sadly crippled by the manacles of segregation and the chains of discrimination. One hundred years later, the Negro lives on a lonely island of poverty in the midst of a vast ocean of material prosperity. One hundred years later, the Negro is still languished in the corners of American society and finds himself an exile in his own land. And so we've come here today to dramatize a shameful condition.

In a sense we've come to our nation's capital to cash a check. When the architects of our republic wrote the magnificent words of the Constitution and the Declaration of Independence, they were signing a promissory note to which every American was to fall heir. This note was a promise that all men, yes, black men as well as white men, would be guaranteed the 'unalienable Rights' of 'Life, Liberty and the pursuit of Happiness'. It is obvious today that America has defaulted on this promissory note, insofar as her citizens of colour are concerned. Instead of honouring this sacred obligation, America has given the Negro people a bad check, a check which has come back marked 'insufficient funds'. But we refuse to believe that the bank of justice is bankrupt. We refuse to believe that there are insufficient funds in the great vaults of opportunity of this nation. And so, we've come to cash this check, a check that will give us upon demand the riches of freedom and the security of justice.

We have also come to this hallowed spot to remind America of the fierce urgency of Now. This is no time to engage in the luxury of cooling off or to take the tranquilizing drug of gradualism. Now is the time to make real the promises of democracy. Now is the time to rise from the dark and desolate valley of segregation to the sunlit path of racial justice. Now is the time to lift our nation from the quicksands of racial injustice to the solid rock of brotherhood. Now is the time to make justice a reality for all of God's children.

It would be fatal for the nation to overlook the urgency of the moment. This sweltering summer of the Negro's legitimate discontent will not pass until there is an invigorating autumn of freedom and equality. 1963 is not an end, but a beginning. And those who hope that the Negro needed to blow off steam and will now be content will have a rude awakening if the nation returns to business as usual. And there will be neither rest nor tranquility in America until the Negro is granted his citizenship rights. The whirlwinds of revolt will continue to shake the foundations of our nation until the bright day of justice emerges.

But there is something that I must say to my people, who

stand on the warm threshold which leads into the palace of justice: in the process of gaining our rightful place, we must not be guilty of wrongful deeds. Let us not seek to satisfy our thirst for freedom by drinking from the cup of bitterness and hatred. We must forever conduct our struggle on the high plane of dignity and discipline. We must not allow our creative protest to degenerate into physical violence. Again and again, we must rise to the majestic heights of meeting physical force with soul force.

The marvellous new militancy which has engulfed the Negro community must not lead us to a distrust of all white people, for many of our white brothers, as evidenced by their presence here today, have come to realize that their destiny is tied up with our destiny. And they have come to realize that their freedom is inextricably bound to our freedom.

We cannot walk alone.

And as we walk, we must make the pledge that we shall always march ahead.

We cannot turn back.

There are those who are asking the devotees of civil rights, 'When will you be satisfied?' We can never be satisfied as long as the Negro is the victim of the unspeakable horrors of police brutality. We can never be satisfied as long as our bodies, heavy with the fatigue of travel, cannot gain lodging in the motels of the highways and the hotels of the cities. We cannot be satisfied as long as the negro's basic mobility is from a smaller ghetto to a larger one. We can never be satisfied as long as our children are stripped of their selfhood and robbed of their dignity by signs stating: 'For Whites Only'. We cannot be satisfied as long as a Negro in Mississippi cannot vote and a Negro in New York believes he has nothing for which to vote. No, no, we are not satisfied, and we will not be satisfied until 'justice rolls down like waters, and righteousness like a mighty stream'.

I am not unmindful that some of you have come here out of great trials and tribulations. Some of you have come fresh from narrow jail cells. And some of you have come from areas where your quest—quest for freedom—left you battered by the storms of persecution and staggered by the winds of police brutality. You have been the veterans of creative suffering. Continue to work with the faith that unearned suffering is redemptive. Go back to Mississippi, go back to Alabama, go back to South Carolina, go back to Georgia, go back to Louisiana, go back to the slums and ghettos of our northern cities, knowing that somehow this situation can and will be changed.

Let us not wallow in the valley of despair, I say to you today, my friends.

And so even though we face the difficulties of today and tomorrow, I still have a dream. It is a dream deeply rooted in the American dream.

I have a dream that one day this nation will rise up and live out the true meaning of its creed: 'We hold these truths to be self-evident, that all men are created equal.' I have a dream that one day on the red hills of Georgia, the sons of former slaves and the sons of former slave owners will be able to sit down together at the table of brotherhood.

I have a dream that one day even the state of Mississippi, a state sweltering with the heat of injustice, sweltering with the heat of oppression, will be transformed into an oasis of freedom and justice.

I have a dream that my four little children will one day live in a nation where they will not be judged by the colour of their skin but by the content of their character.

I have a *dream* today!

I have a dream that one day, down in Alabama, with its vicious racists, with its governor having his lips dripping with the words of 'interposition' and 'nullification'—one day right there in Alabama little black boys and black girls will be able to join hands with little white boys and white girls as sisters and brothers.

I have a *dream* today!

I have a dream that one day every valley shall be exalted, and every hill and mountain shall be made low, the rough places will be made plain, and the crooked places will be made straight; 'and the glory of the Lord shall be revealed and all flesh shall see it together'. This is our hope, and this is the faith that I go back to the South with.

With this faith, we will be able to hew out of the mountain of despair a stone of hope. With this faith, we will be able to transform the jangling discords of our nation into a beautiful symphony of brotherhood. With this faith, we will be able to work together, to pray together, to struggle together, to go to jail together, to stand up for freedom together, knowing that we will be free one day.

And this will be the day—this will be the day when all of God's children will be able to sing with new meaning:

My country, 'tis of thee,
Sweet land of liberty,
Of thee I sing;
Land where my fathers died,
Land of the pilgrims' pride,
From ev'ry mountainside
Let freedom ring!

And if America is to be a great nation, this must become true.

And so let freedom ring from the prodigious hilltops of New Hampshire.

Let freedom ring from the mighty mountains of New York.

Let freedom ring from the heightening Alleghenies of Pennsylvania.

Let freedom ring from the snow-capped Rockies of Colorado.

Let freedom ring from the curvaceous slopes of California.

But not only that:

Let freedom ring from Stone Mountain of Georgia.

Let freedom ring from Lookout Mountain of Tennessee.

Let freedom ring from every hill and molehill of Mississippi.

From every mountainside, let freedom ring.

And when this happens, and when we allow freedom ring, when we let it ring from every village and every hamlet, from every state and every city, we will be able to speed up that day when *all* of God's children, black men and white men, Jews and Gentiles, Protestants and Catholics, will be able to join hands and sing in the words of the old Negro spiritual:

Free at last! Free at last!

Thank God Almighty, we are free at last!

◆

This speech was delivered by Martin Luther King as his acceptance speech after receiving the Nobel Peace Prize. At the age of thirty-five, Martin Luther King, Jr., was the youngest man to have received the Nobel Peace Prize. When he was informed of the prize money of $54,123 he said he would donate it to further the cause of the civil rights movement. On the evening of 4 April 1968, while standing on the balcony of his motel room in Memphis, Tennessee, where he was to lead a protest march in sympathy with striking garbage workers of that city, he was assassinated.

Acceptance Address for the Nobel Peace Prize*

University of Oslo, Norway
10 December 1964

Your Majesty, Your Royal Highness, Mr President, excellencies, ladies and gentlemen: I accept the Nobel Prize for Peace at a moment when twenty-two million negroes of the United States are engaged in a creative battle to end the long night of racial injustice. I accept this award on behalf of a civil rights movement which is moving with determination and a majestic scorn for risk and danger to establish a reign of freedom and a rule of justice.

I am mindful that only yesterday in Birmingham, Alabama, our children, crying out for brotherhood, were answered with fire hoses, snarling dogs, and even death. I am mindful that only yesterday in Philadelphia, Mississippi, young people seeking to secure the right to vote were brutalized and murdered. I am mindful that debilitating and grinding poverty afflicts my people and chains them to the lowest rung of the economic ladder.

Therefore, I must ask why this prize is awarded to a movement which is beleaguered and committed to unrelenting struggle, and to a movement which has not yet won the very peace and brotherhood which is the essence of the Nobel Prize. After contemplation, I conclude that this award, which I receive on behalf of that movement, is

---

*Source: Nobel Peace Foundation

a profound recognition that non-violence is the answer to the crucial political and moral questions of our time: the need for man to overcome oppression and violence without resorting to violence and oppression.

Civilization and violence are antithetical concepts. Negroes of the United States, following the people of India, have demonstrated that non-violence is not sterile passivity, but a powerful moral force which makes for social transformation. Sooner or later, all the people of the world will have to discover a way to live together in peace, and thereby transform this pending cosmic elegy into a creative psalm of brotherhood. If this is to be achieved, man must evolve for all human conflict a method which rejects revenge, aggression and retaliation. The foundation of such a method is love.

The torturous road which has led from Montgomery, Alabama, to Oslo bears witness to this truth, and this is a road over which millions of Negroes are travelling to find a new sense of dignity. This same road has opened for all Americans a new era of progress and hope. It has led to a new civil rights bill, and it will, I am convinced, be widened and lengthened into a superhighway of justice as Negro and white men in increasing numbers create alliances to overcome their common problems.

I accept this award today with an abiding faith in America and an audacious faith in the future of mankind. I refuse to accept despair as the final response to the ambiguities of history.

I refuse to accept the idea that the 'is-ness' of man's present nature makes him morally incapable of reaching up for the eternal 'ought-ness' that forever confronts him.

I refuse to accept the idea that man is mere flotsam and jetsam in the river of life, unable to influence the unfolding events which surround him.

I refuse to accept the view that mankind is so tragically bound to the starless midnight of racism and war that the bright daybreak of peace and brotherhood can never become a reality.

I refuse to accept the cynical notion that nation after nation must spiral down a militaristic stairway into the hell of nuclear annihilation.

I believe that unarmed truth and unconditional love will have the final word in reality. This is why right, temporarily defeated, is stronger than evil triumphant.

I believe that even amid today's mortar bursts and whining bullets, there is still hope for a brighter tomorrow.

I believe that wounded justice, lying prostrate on the blood-flowing streets of our nations, can be lifted from this dust of shame to reign supreme among the children of men.

I have the audacity to believe that people everywhere can have three meals a day for their bodies, education and culture for their minds, and dignity, equality and freedom for their spirits.

I believe that what self-centred men have torn down, men other-centred can build up.

I still believe that one day mankind will bow before the

altars of God and be crowned triumphant over war and bloodshed and non-violent redemptive goodwill proclaimed the rule of the land. And the lion and the lamb shall lie down together, and every man shall sit under his own vine and fig tree, and none shall be afraid.

I still believe that we shall overcome.

This faith can give us courage to face the uncertainties of the future. It will give our tired feet new strength as we continue our forward stride toward the city of freedom. When our days become dreary with low-hovering clouds and our nights become darker than a thousand midnights, we will know that we are living in the creative turmoil of a genuine civilization struggling to be born.

Today I come to Oslo as a trustee, inspired and with renewed dedication to humanity. I accept this prize on behalf of all men who love peace and brotherhood. I say I come as a trustee, for in the depths of my heart I am aware that this prize is much more than an honour to me personally. Every time I take a flight I am always mindful of the many people who make a successful journey possible, the known pilots and the unknown ground crew. You honour the dedicated pilots of our struggle, who have sat at the controls as the freedom movement soared into orbit. You honour, once again, Chief Lutuli of South Africa, whose struggles with and for his people are still met with the most brutal expression of man's inhumanity to man. You honour the ground crew, without whose labour and sacrifice the jet flights to freedom could never have left the earth.

Most of these people will never make the headlines, and their names will never appear in *Who's Who*. Yet, when years have rolled past and when the blazing light of truth is focused on this marvellous age in which we live, men and women will know and children will be taught that we have a finer land, a better people, a more noble civilization because these humble children of God were willing to suffer for righteousness' sake.

I think Alfred Nobel would know what I mean when I say I accept this award in the spirit of a curator of some precious heirloom which he holds in trust for its true owners: all those to whom truth is beauty, and beauty, truth, and in whose eyes the beauty of genuine brotherhood and peace is more precious than diamonds or silver or gold. Thank you.

♦

On 4 April 1967 Martin Luther King delivered his famous speech at Riverside Church wherein he openly condemned the Vietnam War. He insisted that it was morally imperative for the United States to take radical steps to halt the war through non-violent means since it was affecting the American poor and Vietnamese farmers. It was a powerful and angry speech, and at that time, it was publicly condemned by civil rights activists.

Beyond Vietnam : A Time to Break Silence

Riverside Church, New York
4 April 1967

Mr Chairman, ladies and gentlemen, I need not pause to say how very delighted I am to be here tonight, and how very delighted I am to see you expressing your concern about the issues that will be discussed tonight by turning out in such large numbers. I also want to say that I consider it a great honour to share this programme with Dr Bennett, Dr Commager, and Rabbi Heschel, some of the most distinguished leaders and personalities of our nation. And of course it's always good to come back to Riverside Church. Over the last eight years, I have had the privilege of preaching here almost every year in that period, and it's always a rich and rewarding experience to come to this great church and this great pulpit.

I come to this great magnificent house of worship tonight because my conscience leaves me no other choice. I join you in this meeting because I am in deepest agreement with the aims and work of the organization that brought us together, Clergy and Laymen Concerned About Vietnam. The recent statements of your executive committee are the sentiments of my own heart, and I found myself in full accord when I read its opening lines: 'A time comes when silence is betrayal.' That time has come for us in relation to Vietnam.

The truth of these words is beyond doubt, but the mission to which they call us is a most difficult one. Even when pressed by the demands of inner truth, men do not easily assume the task of opposing their government's policy, especially in time of war. Nor does the human spirit move without great difficulty against all the apathy of conformist thought within one's own bosom and in the surrounding world. Moreover, when the issues at hand seem as perplexing as they often do in the case of this dreadful conflict, we are always on the verge of being mesmerized by uncertainty. But we must move on.

Some of us who have already begun to break the silence of the night have found that the calling to speak is often a vocation of agony, but we must speak. We must speak with all the humility that is appropriate to our limited vision, but we must speak. And we must rejoice as well, for surely this is the first time in our nation's history that a significant number of its religious leaders have chosen to move beyond the prophesying of smooth patriotism to the high grounds of a firm dissent based upon the mandates of conscience and the reading of history. Perhaps a new spirit is rising among us. If it is, let us trace its movement, and pray that our inner being may be sensitive to its guidance. For we are deeply in need of a new way beyond the darkness that seems so close around us.

Over the past two years, as I have moved to break the betrayal of my own silences and to speak from the burnings of my own heart, as I have called for radical departures from the destruction of Vietnam, many persons have questioned me about the wisdom of my path. At the heart of their concerns, this query has often loomed large and loud: 'Why are you speaking about the war, Dr King? Why are you joining the voices of dissent?' 'Peace and civil rights don't mix,' they say. 'Aren't you hurting the cause of your people?' they ask. And when I hear them, though I often understand the source of their concern, I am nevertheless greatly saddened, for such questions mean that the inquirers have not really known me, my commitment, or my calling. Indeed, their questions suggest that they do not know the world in which they live. In the light of such tragic misunderstanding, I deem it of signal importance to state clearly, and I trust concisely, why I believe that the path from Dexter Avenue Baptist Church—the church in Montgomery, Alabama, where I began my pastorate—leads clearly to this sanctuary tonight.

I come to this platform tonight to make a passionate plea to my beloved nation. This speech is not addressed to Hanoi or to the National Liberation Front. It is not addressed to China or to Russia. Nor is it an attempt to overlook the ambiguity of the total situation and the need for a collective solution to the tragedy of Vietnam. Neither is it an attempt to make North Vietnam or the National Liberation Front paragons of virtue, nor to overlook the role they must play in the successful resolution of the problem. While they both may have justifiable reasons to be suspicious of the good faith of the United States, life and history give eloquent testimony to the fact that conflicts are never resolved without trustful give and take on both sides. Tonight, however, I wish not to speak with Hanoi and the National Liberation Front, but rather to my fellow Americans.

Since I am a preacher by calling, I suppose it is not surprising that I have seven major reasons for bringing Vietnam into the field of my moral vision. There is at the outset a very obvious and almost facile connection between the war in Vietnam and the struggle I and others have been waging in America. A few years ago there was a shining moment in that struggle. It seemed as if there was a real promise of hope for the poor, both black and white, through the poverty programme. There were experiments, hopes, new beginnings. Then came the buildup in Vietnam, and I watched this programme broken and eviscerated as if it were some idle political plaything on a society gone mad on war. And I knew that America would never invest the necessary funds or energies in rehabilitation of its poor so long as adventures like Vietnam continued to draw men and skills and money like some demonic, destructive suction tube. So I was increasingly compelled to see the war as an enemy of the poor and to attack it as such.

Perhaps a more tragic recognition of reality took place when it became clear to me that the war was doing far more than devastating the hopes of the poor at home. It was sending their sons and their brothers and their husbands to fight and to die in extraordinarily high proportions relative to the rest of the population. We were taking the black young men who had been crippled by our society and sending them eight thousand miles away to guarantee liberties in Southeast Asia which they had not found in southwest Georgia and East Harlem. So we have been repeatedly faced with the cruel irony of watching Negro and white boys on TV screens as they kill and die together for a nation that has been unable to seat them together in the same schools. So we watch them in brutal solidarity burning the huts of a poor village, but we realize that they would hardly live on the same block in Chicago. I could not be silent in the face of such cruel manipulation of the poor.

My third reason moves to an even deeper level of awareness, for it grows out of my experience in the ghettos of the North over the last three years, especially the last three summers. As I have walked among the desperate, rejected, and angry young men, I have told them that Molotov cocktails and rifles would not solve their problems. I have tried to offer them my deepest compassion while maintaining my conviction that social change comes most meaningfully through non-violent action. But they asked, and rightly so, 'What about Vietnam?' They asked if our own nation wasn't using massive doses of violence to solve its problems, to bring about the changes it wanted. Their questions hit home, and I knew that I could never again raise my voice against the violence of the oppressed in the ghettos without having first spoken clearly to the greatest purveyor of violence in the world today: my own government. For the sake of those boys, for the sake of this government, for the sake of the hundreds of thousands trembling under our violence, I cannot be silent.

For those who ask the question, 'Aren't you a civil rights leader?' and thereby mean to exclude me from the movement for peace, I have this further answer. In 1957, when a group of us formed the Southern Christian Leadership Conference, we chose as our motto: 'To save the soul of America'. We were convinced that we could not limit our vision to certain rights for black people, but instead affirmed the conviction that America would never be free or saved from itself until the descendants of its slaves were loosed completely from the shackles they still wear. In a way we were agreeing with Langston Hughes, that black bard of Harlem, who had written earlier:

> O, yes, I say it plain,
> America never was America to me,
> And yet I swear this oath—
> America will be!

Now it should be incandescently clear that no one who has any concern for the integrity and life of America today can ignore the present war. If America's soul becomes totally poisoned, part of the autopsy must read 'Vietnam'. It can never be saved so long as it destroys the deepest hopes of men the world over. So it is that those of us who are yet determined that 'America will be' are led down the path of protest and dissent, working for the health of our land.

As if the weight of such a commitment to the life and

health of America were not enough, another burden of responsibility was placed upon me in 1954.[*] And I cannot forget that the Nobel Peace Prize was also a commission, a commission to work harder than I had ever worked before for the brotherhood of man. This is a calling that takes me beyond national allegiances.

But even if it were not present, I would yet have to live with the meaning of my commitment to the ministry of Jesus Christ. To me, the relationship of this ministry to the making of peace is so obvious that I sometimes marvel at those who ask me why I am speaking against the war. Could it be that they do not know that the Good News was meant for all men—for communist and capitalist, for their children and ours, for black and for white, for revolutionary and conservative? Have they forgotten that my ministry is in obedience to the one who loved his enemies so fully that he died for them? What then can I say to the Vietcong or to Castro or to Mao as a faithful minister of this one? Can I threaten them with death or must I not share with them my life?

Finally, as I try to explain for you and for myself the road that leads from Montgomery to this place, I would have offered all that was most valid if I simply said that I must be true to my conviction that I share with all men the calling to be a son of the living God. Beyond the calling of race or nation or creed is this vocation of sonship and

---

[*]King says '1954', but most likely means 1964, the year he received the Nobel Peace Prize.

brotherhood. Because I believe that the Father is deeply concerned, especially for His suffering and helpless and outcast children, I come tonight to speak for them. This I believe to be the privilege and the burden of all of us who deem ourselves bound by allegiances and loyalties which are broader and deeper than nationalism and which go beyond our nation's self-defined goals and positions. We are called to speak for the weak, for the voiceless, for the victims of our nation, for those it calls 'enemy', for no document from human hands can make these humans any less our brothers.

And as I ponder the madness of Vietnam and search within myself for ways to understand and respond in compassion, my mind goes constantly to the people of that peninsula. I speak now not of the soldiers of each side, not of the ideologies of the Liberation Front, not of the junta in Saigon, but simply of the people who have been living under the curse of war for almost three continuous decades now. I think of them, too, because it is clear to me that there will be no meaningful solution there until some attempt is made to know them and hear their broken cries.

They must see Americans as strange liberators. The Vietnamese people proclaimed their own independence in 1954—in 1945 rather—after a combined French and Japanese occupation and before the communist revolution in China. They were led by Ho Chi Minh. Even though they quoted the American Declaration of Independence in their own document of freedom, we refused to recognize them. Instead, we decided to support France in its reconquest of her former colony. Our government felt then that the Vietnamese people were not ready for independence, and we again fell victim to the deadly Western arrogance that has poisoned the international atmosphere for so long. With that tragic decision we rejected a revolutionary government seeking self-determination and a government that had been established not by China—for whom the Vietnamese have no great love—but by clearly indigenous forces that included some communists. For the peasants this new government meant real land reform, one of the most important needs in their lives.

For nine years following 1945 we denied the people of Vietnam the right of independence. For nine years we vigorously supported the French in their abortive effort to recolonize Vietnam. Before the end of the war we were meeting 80 per cent of the French war costs. Even before the French were defeated at Dien Bien Phu, they began to despair of their reckless action, but we did not. We encouraged them with our huge financial and military supplies to continue the war even after they had lost the will. Soon we would be paying almost the full costs of this tragic attempt at recolonization.

After the French were defeated, it looked as if independence and land reform would come again through the Geneva Agreement. But instead there came the United States, determined that Ho should not unify the temporarily divided nation, and the peasants watched again as we supported one of the most vicious modern dictators, our chosen man, Premier Diem. The peasants watched and cringed and Diem ruthlessly rooted out all opposition, supported their extortionist landlords, and refused even to discuss reunification with the North. The peasants watched as all of this was presided over by United States influence and then by increasing numbers of United States troops who came to help quell the insurgency that Diem's methods had aroused. When Diem was overthrown they may have been happy, but the long line of military dictators seemed to offer no real change, especially in terms of their need for land and peace.

The only change came from America as we increased our troop commitments in support of governments which were singularly corrupt, inept, and without popular support. All the while the people read our leaflets and received the regular promises of peace and democracy and land reform. Now they languish under our bombs and consider us, not their fellow Vietnamese, the real enemy. They move sadly and apathetically as we herd them off the land of their fathers into concentration camps where minimal social needs are rarely met. They know they must move on or be destroyed by our bombs.

So they go, primarily women and children and the aged. They watch as we poison their water, as we kill a million acres of their crops. They must weep as the bulldozers roar through their areas preparing to destroy the precious trees. They wander into the hospitals with at least twenty casualties from American firepower for one Vietcong-inflicted injury. So far we may have killed a million of them, mostly children. They wander into the towns and see thousands of the children, homeless, without clothes, running in packs on the streets like animals. They see the children degraded by our soldiers as they beg for food. They see the children selling their sisters to our soldiers, soliciting for their mothers.

What do the peasants think as we ally ourselves with the landlords and as we refuse to put any action into our many words concerning land reform? What do they think as we test out our latest weapons on them, just as the Germans tested out new medicine and new tortures in the concentration camps of Europe? Where are the roots of the independent Vietnam we claim to be building? Is it among these voiceless ones?

We have destroyed their two most cherished institutions: the family and the village. We have destroyed their land and their crops. We have cooperated in the crushing of the nation's only non-communist revolutionary political force, the unified Buddhist Church. We have supported the enemies of the peasants of Saigon. We have corrupted their women and children and killed their men.

Now there is little left to build on, save bitterness. Soon the only solid physical foundations remaining will be found at our military bases and in the concrete of the concentration camps we call 'fortified hamlets'. The peasants may well wonder if we plan to build our new Vietnam on such grounds as these. Could we blame them for such thoughts? We must speak for them and raise the questions they cannot raise. These, too, are our brothers.

Perhaps a more difficult but no less necessary task is to speak for those who have been designated as our enemies. What of the National Liberation front, that strangely anonymous group we call 'VC' or 'communists'? What must they think of the United States of America when they realize that we permitted the repression and cruelty of Diem, which helped to bring them into being as a resistance group in the South? What do they think of our condoning the violence which led to their own taking up of arms? How can they believe in our integrity when now we speak of 'aggression from the North' as if there was nothing more essential to the war? How can they trust us when now we charge them with violence after the murderous reign of Diem and charge them with violence while we pour every new weapon of death into their land? Surely we must understand their feelings, even if we do not condone their actions. Surely we must see that the men we supported pressed them to their violence. Surely we must see that our own computerized plans of destruction simply dwarf their greatest acts.

How do they judge us when our officials know that their membership is less than 25 per cent communist, and yet insist on giving them the blanket name? What must they be thinking when they know that we are aware of their control of major sections of Vietnam, and yet we appear ready to allow national elections in which this highly organized political parallel government will not have a part? They ask how we can speak of free elections when the Saigon press is censored and controlled by the military junta. And they are surely right to wonder what kind of new government we plan to help form without them, the only real party in real touch with the peasants. They question our political goals and they deny the reality of a peace settlement from which they will be excluded. Their questions are frighteningly relevant. Is our nation planning to build on political myth again, and then shore it up upon the power of a new violence?

Here is the true meaning and value of compassion and non-violence, when it helps us to see the enemy's point of view, to hear his questions, to know his assessment of ourselves. For from his view we may indeed see the basic weaknesses of our own condition, and if we are mature, we may learn and grow and profit from the wisdom of the brothers who are called the opposition.

So, too, with Hanoi. In the North, where our bombs now pummel the land, and our mines endanger the waterways, we are met by a deep but understandable mistrust. To speak for them is to explain this lack of confidence in Western worlds, and especially their distrust of American intentions now. In Hanoi are the men who led this nation to independence against the Japanese and the French, the men who sought membership in the French Commonwealth and were betrayed by the weakness of Paris and the wilfulness of the colonial armies. It was they who led a second struggle against French domination at tremendous costs, and then were persuaded to give up the land they controlled between the thirteenth and seventeenth parallel as a temporary measure at Geneva. After 1954 they watched us conspire with Diem to prevent elections which could have surely brought Ho Chi Minh to power over a unified Vietnam, and they realized they had been betrayed again. When we ask why they do not leap to negotiate, these things must be considered.

Also, it must be clear that the leaders of Hanoi considered the presence of American troops in support of the Diem regime to have been the initial military breach of the Geneva Agreement concerning foreign troops. They remind us that they did not begin to send troops in large numbers and even supplies into the South until American forces had moved into the tens of thousands.

Hanoi remembers how our leaders refused to tell us the truth about the earlier North Vietnamese overtures for peace, how the president claimed that none existed when they had clearly been made. Ho Chi Minh has watched as America has spoken of peace and built up its forces, and now he has surely heard the increasing international rumours of American plans for an invasion of the north. He knows the bombing and shelling and mining we are doing are part of traditional pre-invasion strategy. Perhaps only his sense of humour and of irony can save him when he hears the most powerful nation of the world speaking of aggression as it drops thousands of bombs on a poor, weak nation more than eight hundred, or rather, eight thousand miles away from its shores.

At this point I should make it clear that while I have tried to give a voice to the voiceless in Vietnam and to understand the arguments of those who are called 'enemy', I am as deeply concerned about our own troops there as anything else. For it occurs to me that what we are submitting them to in Vietnam is not simply the brutalizing process that goes on in any war where armies face each other and seek to destroy. We are adding cynicism to the process of death, for they must know after a short period there that none of the things we claim to be fighting for are really involved. Before long they must know that their government has sent them into a struggle among Vietnamese, and the more sophisticated surely realize that we are on the side of the wealthy, and the secure, while we create a hell for the poor.

Surely this madness must cease. We must stop now. I speak as a child of God and brother to the suffering poor of Vietnam. I speak for those whose land is being laid waste, whose homes are being destroyed, whose culture is being subverted. I speak for the poor in America who are paying the double price of smashed hopes at home, and dealt death and corruption in Vietnam. I speak as a citizen of the world, for the world as it stands aghast at the path we have taken. I speak as one who loves America, to the leaders of our own nation. The great initiative in this war is ours; the initiative to stop it must be ours.

This is the message of the great Buddhist leaders of Vietnam. Recently one of them wrote these words, and I quote, 'Each day the war goes on the hatred increases in the hearts of the Vietnamese and in the hearts of those of humanitarian instinct. The Americans are forcing even their friends into becoming their enemies. It is curious that the Americans, who calculate so carefully on the possibilities of military victory do not realize that in the process they are incurring deep psychological and political defeat. The image of America will never again be the image of revolution, freedom, and democracy, but the image of violence and militarism.'

If we continue, there will be no doubt in my mind and in the mind of the world that we have no honourable intentions in Vietnam. If we do not stop our war against the people of Vietnam immediately, the world will be left with no other alternative than to see this as some horrible, clumsy and deadly game we have decided to play. The world now demands a maturity of America that we may not be able to achieve. It demands that we admit we have been wrong from the beginning of our adventure in Vietnam, that we have been detrimental to the life of the Vietnamese people. The situation is one in which we must be ready to turn sharply from our present ways. In order to atone for our sins and errors in Vietnam, we should take the initiative in bringing a halt to this tragic war.

I would like to suggest five concrete things that our government should do to begin the long and difficult process of extricating ourselves from this nightmarish conflict:

Number One: End all bombing in North and South Vietnam.

Number Two: Declare a unilateral ceasefire in the hope that such action will create the atmosphere for negotiation.

Number Three: Take immediate steps to prevent other battlegrounds in Southeast Asia by curtailing our military buildup in Thailand and our interference in Laos.

Number Four: Realistically accept the fact that the National Liberation Front has substantial support in South Vietnam and must thereby play a role in any meaningful negotiations and any future Vietnam government.

Number Five: Set a date that we will remove all foreign troops from Vietnam in accordance with the 1954 Geneva Agreement.

Part of our ongoing commitment might well express itself in an offer to grant asylum to any Vietnamese who fears for his life under a new regime which include the Liberation Front. Then we must make what reparations we can for the damage we have done. We must provide the medical aid that is badly needed, making it available in this country if necessary. Meanwhile, we in the churches and synagogues have a continuing task while we urge our government to disengage itself from a disgraceful commitment. We must continue to raise our voices and our lives if our nation persists in its perverse ways in Vietnam. We must be prepared to match actions with words by seeking out every creative method of protest possible.

As we counsel young men concerning military service, we must clarify for them our nation's role in Vietnam and challenge them with the alternative of conscientious objection. I am pleased to say that this is a path now chosen by more than seventy students at my own alma mater, Morehouse College, and I recommend it to all who find the American course in Vietnam a dishonourable and unjust one. Moreover, I would encourage all ministers of draft age to give up their ministerial exemptions and seek status as conscientious objectors. These are the times for real choices and not false ones. We are at the moment when our lives must be placed on the line if our nation is to survive its own folly. Every man of humane convictions must decide on the protest that best suits his convictions, but we must all protest.

Now there is something seductively tempting about stopping there and sending us all off on what in some circles has become a popular crusade against the war in Vietnam. I say we must enter that struggle, but I wish to go on now to say something even more disturbing.

The war in Vietnam is but a symptom of a far deeper malady within the American spirit, and if we ignore this sobering reality, we will find ourselves organizing 'clergy and laymen concerned' committees for the next generation. They will be concerned about Guatemala and Peru. They will be concerned about Thailand and Cambodia. They will be concerned about Mozambique and South Africa. We will be marching for these and a dozen other names and attending rallies without end unless there is a significant and profound change in American life and policy. So such thoughts take us beyond Vietnam, but not beyond our calling as sons of the living God.

In 1957 a sensitive American official overseas said that it seemed to him that our nation was on the wrong side of a world revolution. During the past ten years we have seen emerge a pattern of suppression which has now justified the presence of U.S. military advisors in Venezuela. This need to maintain social stability for our investments accounts for the counterrevolutionary action of American forces in Guatemala. It tells why American helicopters are being used against guerrillas in Cambodia and why American napalm and Green Beret forces have already been active against rebels in Peru.

It is with such activity that the words of the late John F. Kennedy come back to haunt us. Five years ago he said, 'Those who make peaceful revolution impossible will make violent revolution inevitable.' Increasingly, by choice or by accident, this is the role our nation has taken, the role of those who make peaceful revolution impossible by refusing to give up the privileges and the pleasures that come from the immense profits of overseas investments. I am convinced that if we are to get on to the right side of the world revolution, we as a nation must undergo a radical revolution of values. We must rapidly begin the shift from a thing-oriented society to a person-oriented society. When machines and computers, profit motives and property rights, are considered more important than people, the giant triplets of racism, extreme materialism and militarism are incapable of being conquered.

A true revolution of values will soon cause us to question the fairness and justice of many of our past and present policies. On the one hand we are called to play the Good Samaritan on life's roadside, but that will be only an initial act. One day we must come to see that the whole Jericho Road must be transformed so that men and women will not be constantly beaten and robbed as they make their journey on life's highway. True compassion is more than flinging a coin to a beggar. It comes to see than an edifice which produces beggars needs restructuring.

A true revolution of values will soon look uneasily on the glaring contrast of poverty and wealth. With righteous indignation, it will look across the seas and see individual capitalists of the West investing huge sums of money in Asia, Africa and South America, only to take the profits out with no concern for the social betterment of the countries, and say, 'This is not just.' It will look at our alliance with the landed gentry of South America and say, 'This is not just.' The Western arrogance of feeling that it has everything to teach others and nothing to learn from them is not just.

A true revolution of values will lay hand on the world order and say of war, 'This way of settling differences is not just.' This business of burning human beings with napalm, of filling our nation's homes with orphans and widows, of injecting poisonous drugs of hate into the veins of people normally humane, of sending men home from dark and bloody battlefields physically handicapped and psychologically deranged, cannot be reconciled with wisdom, justice and love. A nation that continues year after year to spend more money on military defence than on programmes of social uplift is approaching spiritual death.

America, the richest and most powerful nation in the world, can well lead the way in this revolution of values. There is nothing except a tragic death wish to prevent us from reordering our priorities so that the pursuit of peace will take precedence over the pursuit of war. There is nothing to keep us from moulding a recalcitrant status quo with bruised hands until we have fashioned it into a brotherhood.

This kind of positive revolution of values is our best defence against communism. War is not the answer. Communism will never be defeated by the use of atomic bombs or nuclear weapons. Let us not join those who shout war and, through their misguided passions, urge the United States to relinquish its participation in the United Nations. These are days which demand wise restraint and calm reasonableness. We must not engage in a negative anticommunism, but rather in a positive thrust for democracy, realizing that our greatest defence against communism is to take offensive action in behalf of justice. We must with positive action seek to remove those conditions of poverty, insecurity, and injustice, which are the fertile soil in which the seed of communism grows and develops.

These are revolutionary times. All over the globe men are revolting against old systems of exploitation and oppression, and out of the wounds of a frail world, new systems of justice and equality are being born. The shirtless and barefoot people of the land are rising up as never before. The people who sat in darkness have seen a great light. We in the West must support these revolutions.

It is a sad fact that because of comfort, complacency, a morbid fear of communism, and our proneness to adjust to injustice, the Western nations that initiated so much of the revolutionary spirit of the modern world have now become the arch anti-revolutionaries. This has driven many to feel that only Marxism has a revolutionary spirit. Therefore, communism is a judgement against our failure to make democracy real and follow through on the revolutions that we initiated. Our only hope today lies in our ability to recapture the revolutionary spirit and go out into a sometimes hostile world declaring eternal hostility to poverty, racism and militarism. With this powerful commitment we shall boldly challenge the status quo and unjust mores, and thereby speed the day when 'every valley shall be exalted, and every mountain and hill shall be made low; the crooked shall be made straight, and the rough places plain'. A genuine revolution of values means in the final analysis that our loyalties must become ecumenical rather than sectional. Every nation must now develop an overriding loyalty to mankind as a whole in order to preserve the best in their individual societies.

This call for a worldwide fellowship that lifts neighbourly concern beyond one's tribe, race, class and nation is in reality a call for an all-embracing and unconditional love for all mankind. This oft misunderstood, this oft misinterpreted concept, so readily dismissed by the Nietzsches of the world as a weak and cowardly force, has now become an absolute necessity for the survival of man. When I speak of love I am not speaking of some sentimental and weak response. I'm not speaking of that force which is just emotional bosh. I am speaking of that force which all of the great religions have seen as the supreme unifying principle of life. Love is somehow the key that unlocks the door which leads to ultimate reality. This Hindu-Muslim-Christian-Jewish-Buddhist belief about ultimate reality is beautifully summed up in the first epistle of Saint John: 'Let us love one another, for love is God. And every one that loveth is born of God and knoweth God. He that loveth not knoweth not God, for God is love... If we love one another, God dwelleth in us and his love is perfected in us.' Let us hope that this spirit will become the order of the day.

We can no longer afford to worship the god of hate or bow before the altar of retaliation. The oceans of history are made turbulent by the ever-rising tides of hate. History is cluttered with the wreckage of nations and individuals that pursued this self-defeating path of hate. As Arnold Toynbee says: 'Love is the ultimate force that makes for the saving choice of life and good against the damning choice of death and evil. Therefore the first hope in our inventory must be the hope that love is going to have the last word.' We are now faced with the fact, my friends, that tomorrow is today. We are confronted with the fierce urgency of now. In this unfolding conundrum of life and history, there is such a thing as being too late. Procrastination is still the thief of time. Life often leaves us standing bare, naked and dejected with a lost opportunity. The tide in the affairs of men does not remain at flood—it ebbs. We may cry out desperately for time to pause in her passage, but time is adamant to every plea and rushes on. Over the bleached bones and jumbled residues of numerous civilizations are written the pathetic words, 'Too late.' There is an invisible book of life that faithfully records our vigilance or our neglect. Omar Khayyam is right: 'The moving finger writes, and having writ moves on.'

We still have a choice today: non-violent coexistence or violent co-annihilation. We must move past indecision to action. We must find new ways to speak for peace in Vietnam and justice throughout the developing world, a world that borders on our doors. If we do not act, we shall surely be dragged down the long, dark and shameful corridors of time reserved for those who possess power without compassion, might without morality, and strength without sight.

Now let us begin. Now let us rededicate ourselves to the long and bitter, but beautiful, struggle for a new world. This is the calling of the sons of God, and our brothers wait eagerly for our response. Shall we say the odds are too great? Shall we tell them the struggle is too hard? Will our message be that the forces of American life militate against their arrival as full men, and we send our deepest regrets? Or will there be another message—of longing, of hope, of solidarity with their yearnings, of commitment to their cause, whatever the cost? The choice is ours, and though we might prefer it otherwise, we must choose in this crucial moment of human history.

As that noble bard of yesterday, James Russell Lowell, eloquently stated:

> Once to every man and nation comes a moment
> to decide,
> In the strife of truth and falsehood, for the good
> or evil side;
> Some great cause, God's new Messiah offering each
> the bloom or blight,
> And the choice goes by forever 'twixt that darkness
> and that light.
> Though the cause of evil prosper, yet 'tis truth alone
> is strong
> Though her portions be the scaffold, and upon the
> throne be wrong
> Yet that scaffold sways the future, and behind the
> dim unknown
> Standeth God within the shadow, keeping watch
> above his own.

And if we will only make the right choice, we will be able to transform this pending cosmic elegy into a creative psalm of peace. If we will make the right choice, we will be able to transform the jangling discords of our world into a beautiful symphony of brotherhood. If we will but make the right choice, we will be able to speed up the day, all over America and all over the world, when justice will roll down like waters, and righteousness like a mighty stream.

8

M . K . Gandhi

'I wanted to avoid violence. Non-violence is the first article of my faith. It is also the last article of my creed.'

ᠬ

The historical trial of Mahatma Gandhi and Shri Shankarlal Ghelabhai Banker, editor, and printer and publisher respectively of Young India, *on charges under Section 124 A of the Indian Penal Code, was held on Saturday, 18 March 1922, before Mr C.N. Broomfield, I.C.S., District and Sessions Judge, Ahmedabad.*

Statement in the Great Trial of 1922

Ahmedabad
18 March 1922

Sir J.T. Strangman, Advocate-General, with Rao Bahadur

Girdharlal Uttamram, Public Prosecutor of Ahmedabad, appeared for the Crown. Mr A.C. Wild, Remembrancer of Legal Affairs, was also present. Mahatma Gandhi and Shri Shankarlal Banker were undefended.

Among the members of the public who were present on the occasion were: Kasturba Gandhi, Sarojini Naidu, Pandit M.M. Malaviya, Shri N.C. Kelkar, Smt J.B. Petit and Smt Anasuyaben Sarabhai.

The Judge, who took his seat at 12 noon, said that there was a slight mistake in the charges which were then read out by the Registrar. These charges were of 'bringing or attempting to excite disaffection towards His Majesty's Government established by law in British India, and thereby committing offences punishable under Section 124 A of the Indian Penal Code', the offences being in three articles published in Young India of September 29 and December 15 of 1921, and February 23 of 1922. The offending articles were then read out: first of them was, 'Tampering with Loyalty'; and second, 'The Puzzle and its Solution', and the last was 'Shaking the Manes'.

The Judge said that the law required that the charges should not be read out but explained. In this case it would not be necessary for him to say much by way of explanation. The charge in each case was that of bringing or attempting to excite into hatred or contempt or exciting or attempting to excite disaffection towards His Majesty's Government, established by law in British India. Both the accused were charged with the three offences under Section 124 A, contained in the articles read out, written by Mahatma Gandhi and printed by Shri Banker.

The charges having been read out, the Judge called upon the accused to plead to the charges. He asked Gandhiji whether he pleaded guilty or claimed to be tried.

Gandhiji: 'I plead guilty to all the charges. I observe that the King's name has been omitted from the charge, and it has been properly omitted.'

The Judge asked Shri Banker the same question and he too readily pleaded guilty.

The Judge wished to give his verdict immediately after Gandhiji had pleaded guilty, but Sir Strangman insisted that the procedure should be carried out in full. The Advocate-General requested the Judge to take into account 'the occurrences in Bombay, Malabar and Chauri Chaura, leading to rioting and murder'. He admitted, indeed, that 'in these articles you find that non-violence is insisted upon as an item of the campaign and of the creed', but the added 'of what value is it to insist on non-violence, if incessantly you preach disaffection towards the Government and hold it up as a treacherous Government, and if you openly and deliberately seek to instigate others to overthrow it'? These were the circumstances which he asked the Judge to take into account in passing sentence on the accused.

As regards Shri Banker, the second accused, the offence was lesser. He did the publication but did not write. Sir Strangman's instructions were that Shri Banker was a man of means and he requested the court to impose a substantial fine in addition to such term of imprisonment as might be inflicted upon.

Court: Mr Gandhi, do you wish to make any statement on the question of sentence?

Gandhiji: I would like to make a statement.

Court: Could you give me in writing to put it on record?

Gandhiji: I shall give it as soon as I finish it.

[Gandhiji then made the following oral statement followed by a written statement that he read.]

Before I read this statement I would like to state that I entirely endorse the learned Advocate-General's remarks in connection with my humble self. I think that he has made, because it is very true and I have no desire whatsoever to conceal from this court the fact that to preach disaffection towards the existing system of Government has become almost a passion with me, and the Advocate-General is entirely in the right when he says that my preaching of disaffection did not commence with my connection with Young India but that it commenced much earlier, and in the statement that I am about to read, it will be my painful duty to admit before this court that it commenced much earlier than the period stated by the Advocate-General. It is a painful duty with me but I have to discharge that duty knowing the responsibility that rests upon my shoulders, and I wish to endorse all the blame that the learned Advocate-General has thrown on my shoulders in connection with the Bombay occurrences, Madras occurrences and the Chauri Chaura occurrences. Thinking over these things deeply and sleeping over them night after night, it is impossible for me to dissociate myself from the diabolical crimes of Chauri Chaura or the mad outrages of Bombay. He is quite right when he says, that as a man of responsibility, a man having received a fair share of education, having had a fair share of experience of this world, I should have known the consequences of every one of my acts. I know them. I knew that I was playing with fire. I ran the risk and if I was set free I would still do the same. I have felt it this morning that I would have failed in my duty, if I did not say what I said here just now.

I wanted to avoid violence. Non-violence is the first article of my faith. It is also the last article of my creed. But I had to make my choice. I had either to submit to a system which I considered had done an irreparable harm to my country, or incur the risk of the mad fury of my people bursting forth when they understood the truth from my lips. I know that my people have sometimes gone mad. I am deeply sorry for it and I am, therefore, here to submit not to a light penalty but to the highest penalty. I do not ask for mercy. I do not plead any extenuating act. I am here, therefore, to invite and cheerfully submit to the highest penalty that can be inflicted upon me for what in law is a deliberate crime, and what appears to me to be the highest duty of a citizen. The only course open to you, the Judge, is, as I am going to say in my statement, either to resign your post, or inflict on me the severest penalty if you believe that the system and law you are assisting to administer are good for the people. I do not except that kind of conversion. But by the time I have finished with my statement you will have a glimpse of what is raging within my breast to run this maddest risk which a sane man can run.

He then read out the written statement: I owe it perhaps to the Indian public and to the public in England, to placate which this prosecution is mainly taken up, that I should explain why from a staunch loyalist and co-operator, I have become an uncompromising disaffectionist and non-co-operator. To the court too I should say why I plead guilty to the charge of promoting disaffection towards the Government established by law in India.

My public life began in 1893 in South Africa in troubled weather. My first contact with British authority in that country was not of a happy character. I discovered that as a man and an Indian, I had no rights. More correctly I discovered that I had no rights as a man because I was an Indian.

But I was not baffled. I thought that this treatment of Indians was an excrescence upon a system that was intrinsically and mainly good. I gave the Government my voluntary and hearty co-operation, criticizing it freely where I felt it was faulty but never wishing its destruction.

Consequently when the existence of the Empire was threatened in 1899 by the Boer challenge, I offered my services to it, raised a volunteer ambulance corps and served at several actions that took place for the relief of Ladysmith. Similarly in 1906, at the time of the Zulu 'revolt,'

I raised a stretcher bearer party and served till the end of the 'rebellion'. On both the occasions I received medals and was even mentioned in dispatches. For my work in South Africa I was given by Lord Hardinge a Kaisar-i-Hind gold medal. When the war broke out in 1914 between England and Germany, I raised volunteer ambulance cars in London, consisting of the then resident Indians in London, chiefly students. Its work was acknowledged by the authorities to be valuable. Lastly, in India when a special appeal was made at the war Conference in Delhi in 1918 by Lord Chelmsford for recruits, I struggled at the cost of my health to raise a corps in Kheda, and the response was being made when the hostilities ceased and orders were received that no more recruits were wanted. In all these efforts at service, I was actuated by the belief that it was possible by such services to gain a status of full equality in the Empire for my countrymen.

The first shock came in the shape of the Rowlatt Act—a law designed to rob the people of all real freedom. I felt called upon to lead an intensive agitation against it. Then followed the Punjab horrors beginning with the massacre at Jallianwala Bagh and culminating in crawling orders, public flogging and other indescribable humiliations. I discovered too that the plighted word of the Prime Minister to the Mussalmans of India regarding the integrity of Turkey and the holy places of Islam was not likely to be fulfilled. But in spite of the forebodings and the grave warnings of friends, at the Amritsar Congress in 1919, I fought for co-operation and working of the Montagu-Chemlmsford reforms, hoping that the Prime Minister would redeem his promise to the Indian Mussalmans, that the Punjab wound would be healed, and that the reforms, inadequate and unsatisfactory though they were, marked a new era of hope in the life of India.

But all that hope was shattered. The Khilafat promise was not to be redeemed. The Punjab crime was whitewashed and most culprits went not only unpunished but remained in service, and some continued to draw pensions from the Indian revenue and in some cases were even rewarded. I saw too that not only did the reforms not mark a change of heart, but they were only a method of further draining India of her wealth and of prolonging her servitude.

I came reluctantly to the conclusion that the British connection had made India more helpless than she ever was before, politically and economically. A disarmed India has no power of resistance against any aggressor if she wanted to engage in an armed conflict with him. So much is this the case that some of our best men consider that India must take generations before she can achieve Dominion Status. She has become so poor that she has little power of resisting famines. Before the British advent India spun and wove in her millions of cottages, just the supplement she needed for adding to her meagre agricultural resources. This cottage industry, so vital for India's existence, has been ruined by incredibly heartless and inhuman processes as described by English witnesses. Little do town dwellers know how the semi-starved masses of India are slowly sinking to lifelessness. Little do they know that their miserable comfort represents the brokerage they get for their work they do for the foreign exploiter, that the profits and the brokerage are sucked from the masses. Little do they realize that the Government established by law in British India is carried on for this exploitation of the masses. No sophistry, no jugglery in figures, can explain away the evidence that the skeletons in many villages present to the naked eye. I have no doubt whatsoever that both England and the town dweller of India will have to answer, if there is a God above, for this crime against humanity, which is perhaps unequalled in history. The law itself in this country has been used to serve the foreign exploiter. My unbiased examination of the Punjab Marital Law cases has led me to believe that at least ninety-five per cent of convictions were wholly bad. My experience of political cases in India leads me to the conclusion, in nine out of every ten, the condemned men were totally innocent. Their crime consisted in the love of their country. In ninety-nine cases out of hundred, justice has been denied to Indians as against Europeans in the courts of India. This is not an exaggerated picture. It is the experience of almost every Indian who has had anything to do with such cases. In my opinion, the administration of the law is thus prostituted, consciously or unconsciously, for the benefit of the exploiter.

The greater misfortune is that the Englishmen and their Indian associates in the administration of the country do not know that they are engaged in the crime I have attempted to describe. I am satisfied that many Englishmen and Indian officials honestly believe that they are administering one of the best systems devised in the world, and that India is making steady, though, slow progress. They do not know, a subtle but effective system of terrorism and an organized display of force on the one hand, and the deprivation of all powers of retaliation or self-defence on the other, as emasculated the people and induced in them the habit of simulation. This awful habit has added to the ignorance and the self-deception of the administrators. Section 124 A, under which I am happily charged, is perhaps the prince among the political sections of the Indian Penal Code designed to suppress the liberty of the citizen. Affection cannot be manufactured or regulated by law. If one has no affection for a person or system, one should be free to give the fullest expression to his disaffection, so long as he does not contemplate, promote or incite violence. But the section under which mere promotion of disaffection is a crime—I have studied some of the cases tried under it; I know that some of the most loved of India's patriots have been convicted under it. I consider it a privilege, therefore, to be charged under that section. I have endeavoured to give in their briefest outline the reasons for my disaffection. I have no personal ill-will against any single administrator, much less can I have any disaffection towards the King's person. But I hold it to be a virtue to be disaffected towards a Government which in its totality has done more harm to India than any previous system. India is less manly under the British rule than she ever was before. Holding such a belief, I consider it to be a sin to have affection for the system. And it has been a precious privilege for me to be able to write what I have in the various articles tendered in evidence against me.

In fact, I believe that I have rendered a service to India and England by showing in non-co-operation the way out of the unnatural state in which both are living. In my opinion, non-co-operation with evil is as much a duty as is co-operation with good. But in the past, non-co-operation has been deliberately expressed in violence to the evil-doer. I am endeavouring to show to my countrymen that violent non-co-operation only multiples evil, and that as evil can only be sustained by violence, withdrawal of support of evil requires complete abstention from violence. Non-violence implies voluntary submission to the penalty for non-co-operation with evil. I am here, therefore, to invite and submit cheerfully to the highest penalty that can be inflicted upon me for what in law is deliberate crime, and what appears to me to be the highest duty of a citizen. The only course open to you, the Judge and the assessors, is either to resign your posts and thus dissociate yourselves from evil, if you feel that the law you are called upon to administer is an evil, and that in reality I am innocent, or to inflict on me the severest penalty, if you believe that the system and the law you are assisting to administer are good for the people of this country, and that my activity is, therefore, injurious to the common weal.

On 11 March 1930, the crowd swelled to 10,000 at the evening prayer held on the Sabarmati sands at Ahmedabad. At the end, Gandhiji delivered a memorable speech on the eve of his historic march.

Dandi March Speech

Sabarmati Ashram, Gujarat
11 March, 1930

In all probability this will be my last speech to you. Even if the government allows me to march tomorrow morning, this will be my last speech on the sacred banks of the Sabarmati. Possibly these may be the last words of my life here.

I have already told you yesterday what I had to say. Today I shall confine myself to what you should do after my companions and I are arrested. The programme of the march to Jalalpur must be fulfilled as originally settled. The enlistment of the volunteers for this purpose should be confined to Gujarat only. From what I have been and heard during the last fortnight, I am inclined to believe that the stream of civil resisters will flow unbroken.

But let there be not a semblance of breach of peace even after all of us have been arrested. We have resolved to utilize all our resources in the pursuit of an exclusively non-violent struggle. Let no one commit a wrong in anger. This is my hope and prayer. I wish these words of mine reached every nook and corner of the land. My task shall be done if I perish and so do my comrades. It will then be for the Working Committee of the Congress to show you the way and it will be up to you to follow its lead. So long as I have reached Jalalpur, let nothing be done in contravention to the authority vested in me by the Congress. But once I am arrested, the whole responsibility shifts to the Congress. No one who believes in non-violence, as a creed, need, therefore, sit still. My compact with the Congress ends as soon as I am arrested. In that case, volunteers, wherever possible, civil disobedience of salt should be started. These laws can be violated in three ways. It is an offence to manufacture salt wherever there are facilities for doing so. The possession and sale of contraband salt, which includes natural salt or salt earth, is also an offence. The purchasers of such salt will be equally guilty. To carry away the natural salt deposits on the seashore is likewise violation of law. So is the hawking of such salt. In short, you may choose any one or all of these devices to break the salt monopoly.

We are, however, not to be content with this alone. There is no ban by the Congress and wherever the local workers have self-confidence other suitable measures may be adopted. I stress only one condition, namely, let our pledge of truth and non-violence as the only means for the attainment of Swaraj be faithfully kept. For the rest, everyone has a free hand. But, that does not give a licence to all and sundry to carry on their own responsibility.

WORDS OF GLORY

Wherever there are local leaders, their orders should be obeyed by the people. Where there are no leaders and only a handful of men have faith in the programme, they may do what they can, if they have enough self-confidence. They have a right, nay it is their duty, to do so. The history of the world is full of instances of men who rose to leadership, by sheer force of self-confidence, bravery and tenacity. We too, if we sincerely aspire to Swaraj and are impatient to attain it, should have similar self-confidence. Our ranks will swell and our hearts strengthen, as the number of our arrests by the government increases.

Much can be done in many other ways besides these. The liquor and foreign cloth shops can be picketed. We can refuse to pay taxes if we have the requisite strength. The lawyers can give up practice. The public can boycott the law courts by refraining from litigation. Government servants can resign their posts. In the midst of the despair reigning all round people quake with fear of losing employment. Such men are unfit for Swaraj. But why this despair? The number of government servants in the country does not exceed a few hundred thousands. What about the rest? Where are they to go? Even free India will not be able to accommodate a greater number of public servants. A collector then will not need the number of servants he has got today. He will be his own servant. Our starving millions can by no means afford this enormous expenditure. If, therefore, we are sensible enough, let us bid goodbye to government employment, no matter if it is the post of a judge or a peon. Let all who are cooperating with the government in one way or another, be it by paying taxes, keeping titles, or sending children to official schools, etc. withdraw their cooperation in all or as many ways as possible. Then there are women who can stand shoulder to shoulder with men in this struggle.

You may take it as my will. It was the message that I desired to impart to you before starting on the march or for the jail. I wish that there should be no suspension or abandonment of the war that commences tomorrow morning or earlier, if I am arrested before that time. I shall eagerly await the news that ten batches are ready as soon as my batch is arrested. I believe there are men in India to complete the work begun by me. I have faith in the righteousness of our cause and the purity of our weapons. And where the means are clean, there God is undoubtedly present with His blessings. And where these three combine, there defeat is an impossibility. A Satyagrahi, whether free or incarcerated, is ever victorious. He is vanquished only when he forsakes truth and non-violence and turns a deaf ear to the inner voice. If, therefore, there is such a thing as defeat for even a Satyagrahi, he alone is the cause of it. God bless you all and keep off all obstacles from the path in the struggle that begins tomorrow.

♦

Gandhiji addressed the A.I.C.C. at Bombay on 8 August 1942 outlining his plan of action, in Hindustani.

The Quit India Speech

Gowalia Tank Maidan, Bombay
8 August 1942

I

Before you discuss the resolution, let me place before you one or two things. I want you to understand two things very clearly and to consider them from the same point of view from which I am placing them before you. I ask you to consider it from my point of view, because if you approve of it, you will be enjoined to carry out all I say. It will be a great responsibility. There are people who ask me whether I am the same man that I was in 1920, or whether there has been any change in me. You are right in asking that question.

Let me, however, hasten to assure that I am the same Gandhi as I was in 1920. I have not changed in any fundamental respect. I attach the same importance to non-violence that I did then. If at all, my emphasis on it has grown stronger. There is no real contradiction between the present resolution and my previous writings and utterances.

Occasions like the present do not occur in everybody's and but rarely in anybody's life. I want you to know and feel that there is nothing but purest Ahimsa in all that I am saying and doing today. The draft resolution of the Working Committee is based on Ahimsa, the contemplated struggle similarly has its roots in Ahimsa. If, therefore, there is any among you who has lost faith in Ahimsa or is wearied of it, let him not vote for this resolution.

Let me explain my position clearly. God has vouchsafed to me a priceless gift in the weapon of Ahimsa. I and my Ahimsa are on our trail today. If in the present crisis, when the earth is being scorched by the flames of Himsa and crying for deliverance, I failed to make use of the God given talent, God will not forgive me and I shall be judged unwrongly of the great gift. I must act now. I may not hesitate and merely look on, when Russia and China are threatened.

Ours is not a drive for power, but purely a non-violent fight for India's independence. In a violent struggle, a successful general has been often known to effect a military coup and to set up a dictatorship. But under the Congress scheme of things, essentially non-violent as it is, there can be no room for dictatorship. A non-violent soldier of freedom will covet nothing for himself, he fights only for the freedom of his country. The Congress is unconcerned as to who will rule, when freedom is attained. The power, when it comes, will belong to the people of India, and it will be for them to decide to whom it placed in the entrusted. Maybe that the reins will be placed in the hands of the Parsis, for instance—as I would love to see happen—or they may be handed to some others whose names are not heard in the Congress today. It will not be for you then to object, saying, 'This community is microscopic. That party did not play its due part in the freedom struggle; why should it have all the power?' Ever since its inception the Congress has kept itself meticulously free of the communal taint. It has thought always in terms of the whole nation and has acted accordingly... I know how imperfect our Ahimsa is and how far away we are still from the ideal, but in Ahimsa there is no final failure or defeat. I have faith, therefore, that if, in spite of our shortcomings, the big thing does happen, it will be because God wanted to help us by crowning with success our silent, unremitting Sadhana for the last twenty-two years.

I believe that in the history of the world, there has not been a more genuinely democratic struggle for freedom than ours. I read Carlyle's French Resolution while I was in prison, and Pandit Jawaharlal has told me something about the Russian revolution. But it is my conviction that inasmuch as these struggles were fought with the weapon of violence they failed to realize the democratic ideal. In the democracy which I have envisaged, a democracy established by non-violence, there will be equal freedom for all. Everybody will be his own master. It is to join a struggle for such democracy that I invite you today. Once you realize this you will forget the differences between the Hindus and Muslims, and think of yourselves as Indians only, engaged in the common struggle for independence.

Then, there is the question of your attitude towards the British. I have noticed that there is hatred towards the British among the people. The people say they are disgusted with their behaviour. The people make no distinction between British imperialism and the British people. To them, the two are one. This hatred would even make them welcome the Japanese. It is most dangerous. It means that they will exchange one slavery for another. We must get rid of this feeling. Our quarrel is not with the British people, we fight their imperialism. The proposal for the withdrawal of British power did not come out of anger. It came to enable India to play its due part at the present critical juncture. It is not a happy position for a big country like India to be merely helping with money and material obtained willy-nilly from her while the United Nations is conducting the war. We cannot evoke the true spirit of sacrifice and valour, so long as we are not free. I know the British Government will not be able to withhold freedom from us, when we have made enough self-sacrifice. We must, therefore, purge ourselves of hatred. Speaking for myself, I can say that I have never felt any hatred. As a matter of fact, I feel myself to be a greater friend of the British now than ever before. One reason is that they are today in distress. My very friendship, therefore, demands that I should try to save them from their mistakes. As I view the situation, they are on the brink of an abyss. It, therefore, becomes my duty to warn them of their danger even though it may, for the time being, anger them to the point of cutting off the friendly hand that is stretched out to help them. People may laugh, nevertheless that is my claim. At a time when I may have to launch the biggest struggle of my life, I may not harbour hatred against anybody.

II

I congratulate you on the resolution that you have just passed. I also congratulate the three comrades on the courage they have shown in pressing their amendments to a division, even though they knew that there was an overwhelming majority in favour of the resolution, and I congratulate the thirteen friends who voted against the resolution. In doing so, they had nothing to be ashamed of. For the last twenty years we have tried to learn not to lose courage even when we are in a hopeless minority and are laughed at. We have learned to hold on to our beliefs in the confidence that we are in the right. It behoves us to cultivate this courage of conviction, for it ennobles man and raises his moral stature.

I was, therefore, glad to see that these friends had imbibed the principle which I have tried to follow for the last fifty years and more.

Having congratulated them on their courage, let me say that what they asked this Committee to accept through their amendments was not the correct representation of the situation. These friends ought to have pondered over the appeal made to them by the Maulana to withdraw their amendments; they should have carefully followed the explanations given by Jawaharlal. Had they done so, it would have been clear to them that the right which they now want the Congress to concede has already been conceded by the Congress.

Time was when every Mussalman claimed the whole of India as his motherland. During the years that the Ali brothers were with me, the assumption underlying all their talks and discussions was that India belonged as much to the Mussalmans as to the Hindus. I can testify to the fact that this was their innermost conviction and not a mask; I lived with them for years. I spent days and nights in their company. And I make bold to say that their utterances were the honest expression of their beliefs. I know there are some who say that I take things too readily at their face value, that I am gullible. I do not think I am such a simpleton, nor am I so gullible as these friends take me to be. But their criticism does not hurt me. I should prefer to be considered gullible rather than deceitful.

What these Communist friends proposed through their amendments is nothing new. It has been repeated from thousands of platforms. Thousands of Mussalmans have told me, that if the Hindu-Muslim question was to be solved satisfactorily, it must be done in my lifetime. I should feel flattered at this; but how can I agree to a proposal which does not appeal to my reason? Hindu-Muslim unity is not a new thing. Millions of Hindus and Mussalmans have sought after it. I consciously strove for its achievement from my boyhood. While at school, I made it a point to cultivate the friendship of Muslims and Parsi co-students. I believed even at that tender age that the Hindus in India, if they wished to live in peace and amity with the other communities, should assiduously cultivate the virtue of neighbourliness. It did not matter, I felt, if I made no special effort to cultivate the friendship with Hindus, but I must make friends with at least a few Mussalmans. It was as counsel for a Mussalman's merchant that I went to South Africa. I made friends with other Mussalmans there, even with the opponents of my client, and gained a reputation for integrity and good faith. I had among my friends and co-workers Muslims as well as Parsis. I captured their hearts and when I left finally for India, I left them sad and shedding tears of grief at the separation.

In India too I continued my efforts and left no stone unturned to achieve that unity. It was my lifelong aspiration for it that made me offer my fullest cooperation to the Mussalmans in the Khilafat movement. Muslims throughout the country accepted me as their true friend.

How then is it that I have now come to be regarded as so evil and detestable? Had I any axe to grind in supporting the Khilafat movement? True, I did in my heart of hearts cherish a hope that it might enable me to save the cow. I am a worshipper of the cow. I believe the cow and myself to be the creation of the same God, and I am prepared to sacrifice my life in order to save the cow. But, whatever my philosophy of life and my ultimate hopes, I joined the movement in no spirit of bargain. I cooperated in the struggle for the Khilafat solely on order to discharge my obligation to my neighbour who, I saw, was in distress. The Ali brothers, had they been alive today, would have testified to the truth of this assertion. And so would many others bear me out in that it was not a bargain on my part for saving the cow.

The cow, like the Khilafat, stood on her own merits. As an honest man, a true neighbour and a faithful friend, it was incumbent on me to stand by the Mussalmans in the hour of their trial.

In those days, I shocked the Hindus by dining with the Mussalmans, though with the passage of time they have now got used to it. Maulana Bari told me, however, that though he would insist on having me as his guest he would not allow me to dine with him, lest someday he should be accused of a sinister motive. And so, whenever I had occasion to stay with him, he called a Brahmana cook and made social arrangements for separate cooking. Firangi Mahal, his residence, was an old-styled structure with limited accommodation; yet he cheerfully bore all hardships and carried out his resolve from which I could not dislodge him. It was the spirit of courtesy, dignity and nobility that inspired us in those days. They respected one another's religious feelings, and considered it a privilege to do so. Not a trace of suspicion lurked in anybody's heart. Where has all that dignity, that nobility of spirit, disappeared now? I should ask all Mussalmans, including Quaid-i-Azam Jinnah, to recall those glorious days and to find out what has brought us to the present impasse. Quaid-i-Azam Jinnah himself was at one time a Congressman. If today the Congress has incurred his wrath, it is because the canker of suspicion has entered his heart. May God bless him with long life, but when I am gone, he will realize and admit that I had no designs on Mussalmans and that I had never betrayed their interests. Where is the escape for me, if I injure their cause or betray their interests? My life is entirely at their disposal. They are free to put an end to it, whenever they wish to do so. Assaults have been made on my life in the past, but God has spared me till now, and the assailants have repented for their action. But if someone were to shoot me in the belief that he was getting rid of a rascal, he would kill not the real Gandhi, but the one that appeared to him a rascal.

To those who have been indulging in a campaign of abuse and vilification, I would say, 'Islam enjoins you not to revile even an enemy. The Prophet treated even enemies with kindness and tried to win them over by his fairness and generosity. Are you followers of that Islam or of any other? If you are followers of the true Islam, does it behove you to distrust the words of one who makes a public declaration of his faith? You may take it from me that one day you will regret the fact that you distrusted and killed one who was a true and devoted friend of yours.' It cuts me to the quick to see that the more I appeal and the more the Maulana importunes, the more intense does the campaign of vilification grow. To me, these abuses are like bullets. They can kill me, even as a bullet can put an end to my life. You may kill me. That will not hurt me. But what of those who indulge in abusing? They bring discredit to Islam. For the fair name of Islam, I appeal to you to resist this unceasing campaign of abuse and vilification.

Maulana Saheb is being made a target for the filthiest

abuse. Why? Because he refuses to exert on me the pressure of his friendship. He realizes that it is a misuse of friendship to seek up to compel a friend to accept as truth what he knows is an untruth.

To the Quaid-i-Azam I would say: Whatever is true and valid in the claim for Pakistan is already in your hands. What is wrong and untenable is in nobody's gift, so that it can be made over to you. Even if someone were to succeed in imposing an untruth on others, he would not be able to enjoy for long the fruits of such a coercion. God dislikes pride and keeps away from it. God would not tolerate a forcible imposition of an untruth.

The Quaid-i-Azam says that he is compelled to say bitter things but that he cannot help giving expression to his thoughts and his feelings. Similarly I would say: 'I consider myself a friend of Mussalmans. Why should I then not give expression to the things nearest to my heart, even at the cost of displeasing them? How can I conceal my innermost thoughts from them? I should congratulate the Quaid-i-Azam on his frankness in giving expression to his thoughts and feelings, even if they sound bitter to his hearers. But even so why should the Mussalmans sitting here be reviled, if they do not see eye to eye with him? If millions of Mussalmans are with you can you not afford to ignore the handful of Mussalmans who may appear to you to be misguided? Why should one with the following of several millions be afraid of a majority community, or of the minority being swamped by the majority? How did the Prophet work among the Arabs and the Mussalmans? How did he propagate Islam? Did he say he would propagate Islam only when he commanded a majority? I appeal to you for the sake of Islam to ponder over what I say. There is neither fair play nor justice in saying that the Congress must accept a thing, even if it does not believe in it and even if it goes counter to principles it holds dear.

Rajaji said, 'I do not believe in Pakistan. But Mussalmans ask for it, Mr Jinnah asks for it, and it has become an obsession with them. Why not then say 'yes' to them just now? The same Mr Jinnah will later on realize the disadvantages of Pakistan and will forgo the demand.' I said, 'It is not fair to accept as true a thing which I hold to be untrue, and ask others to do so in the belief that the demand will not be pressed when the time comes for settling in finally. If I hold the demand to be just, I should concede it this very day. I should not agree to it merely in order to placate Jinnah Saheb. Many friends have come and asked me to agree to it for the time being to placate Mr Jinnah, disarm his suspicions and to see how he reacts to it. But I cannot be party to a course of action with a false promise. At any rate, it is not my method.'

The Congress has no sanction but the moral one for enforcing its decisions. It believes that true democracy can only be the outcome of non-violence. The structure of a world federation can be raised only on a foundation of non-violence, and violence will have to be totally abjured from world affairs. If this is true, the solution of Hindu-Muslim question, too, cannot be achieved by a resort to violence. If the Hindus tyrannize over the Mussalmans, with what face will they talk of a world federation? It is for the same reason that I do not believe in the possibility of establishing world peace through violence as the English and American statesmen propose to do. The Congress has agreed to submitting all the differences to an impartial international tribunal and to abide by its decisions. If even this fairest of proposals is unacceptable, the only course that remains open is that of the sword, of violence. How can I persuade myself to agree to an impossibility? To demand the vivisection of a living organism is to ask for its very life. It is a call to war. The Congress cannot be party to such a fratricidal war. Those Hindus who, like Dr Moonje and Shri Savarkar, believe in the doctrine of the sword may seek to keep the Mussalmans under Hindus domination. I do not represent that section. I represent the Congress. You want to kill the Congress which is the goose that lays golden eggs. If you distrust the Congress, you may rest assured that there is to be perpetual war between the Hindus and the Mussalmans, and the country will be doomed to continue warfare and bloodshed. If such warfare is to be our lot, I shall not live to witness it.

It is for that reason that I say to Jinnah Saheb, 'You may take it from me that whatever in your demand for Pakistan accords with considerations of justice and equity is lying in your pocket; whatever in the demand is contrary to justice and equity you can take only by the sword and in no other manner.'

There is much in my heart that I would like to pour out before this assembly. One thing which was uppermost in my heart I have already dealt with. You may take it from me that it is with me a matter of life and death. If we Hindus and Mussalmans mean to achieve a heart unity, without the slightest mental reservation on the part of either, we must first unite in the effort to be free from the shackles of this empire. If Pakistan after all is to be a portion of India, what objection can there be for Mussalmans against joining this struggle for India's freedom? The Hindus and Mussalmans must, therefore, unite in the first instance on the issue of fighting for freedom. Jinnah Saheb thinks the war will last long. I do not agree with him. If the war goes on for six months more, how shall we be able to save China?

I, therefore, want freedom immediately, this very night, before dawn, if it can be had. Freedom cannot now wait for the realization of communal unity. If that unity is not achieved, sacrifices necessary for it will have to be much greater than would have otherwise sufficed. But the Congress must win freedom or be wiped out in the effort. And forget not that the freedom which the Congress is struggling to achieve will not be for the Congressmen alone but for all the forty crores of the Indian people. Congressmen must for ever remain humble servants of the people.

The Quaid-i-Azam has said that the Muslim League is prepared to take over the rule from the Britishers if they are prepared to hand it over to the Muslim League, for the British took over the empire from the hands of the Muslims. This, however, will be Muslim Raj. The offer made by Maulana Saheb and by me does not imply establishment of Muslim Raj or Muslim domination. The Congress does not believe in the domination of any group or community. It believes in democracy which includes in its orbit Muslims, Hindus, Christians, Parsis, Jews—every one of the communities inhabiting this vast country. If Muslim Raj is inevitable, then let it be; but how can we give it the stamp of our assent? How can we agree to the domination of one community over the others?

Millions of Mussalmans in this country come from Hindu stock. How can their homeland be any other than India? My eldest son embraced Islam some years back. What would his homeland be—Porbandar or the Punjab? I ask the Mussalmans: 'If India is not your homeland, what other country do you belong to? In what separate homeland would you put my son who embraced Islam?' His mother wrote him a letter after his conversion, asking him if he had on embracing Islam given up drinking which Islam forbids to its follower. To those who gloated over the conversion, she wrote to say: 'I do not mind his becoming a Mussalman, so much as his drinking. Will you, as pious Mussalmans, tolerate his drinking even after his conversion? He has reduced himself to the state of a rake by drinking. If you are going to make a man of him again, his conversion will have been turned to good account. You will, therefore, please see that he as a Mussalman abjures wine and woman. If that change does not come about, his conversion goes in vain and our non-cooperation with him will have to continue.'

India is without doubt the homeland of all the Mussalmans inhabiting this country. Every Mussalman should therefore cooperate in the fight for India's freedom. The Congress does not belong to any one class or community; it belongs to the whole nation. It is open to Mussalmans to take possession of the Congress. They can, if they like, swamp the Congress by their numbers, and can steer it along the course which appeals to them. The Congress is fighting not on behalf of the Hindu but on behalf of the whole nation, including the minorities. It would hurt me to hear of a single instance of a Mussalman being killed by a Congressman. In the coming revolution, Congressmen will sacrifice their lives in order to protect the Mussalman against a Hindu's attack and vice versa. It is a part of their creed, and is one of the essentials of non-violence. You will be expected on occasions like these not to lose your heads. Every Congressman, whether a Hindu or a Mussalman, owes this duty to the organization to which he belongs. The Mussalman who will act in this manner will render a service to Islam. Mutual trust is essential for success in the final nationwide struggle that is to come.

I have said that much greater sacrifice will have to be made this time in the wake of our struggle because of the opposition from the Muslim League and from Englishmen. You have seen the secret circular issued by Sir Frederick Puckle. It is a suicidal course that he has taken. It contains an open incitement to organizations which crop up like mushrooms to combine to fight the Congress. We have thus to deal with an empire whose ways are crooked. Ours is a straight path which we can tread even with our eyes closed. That is the beauty of Satyagraha.

In Satyagraha, there is no place for fraud or falsehood, or any kind of untruth. Fraud and untruth today are stalking the world. I cannot be a helpless witness to such a situation. I have travelled all over India as perhaps nobody in the present age has. The voiceless millions of the land saw in me their friend and representative, and I identified myself with them to an extent it was possible for a human being to do. I saw trust in their eyes, which I now want to turn to good account in fighting this empire upheld on untruth and violence. However gigantic the preparations that the empire has made, we must get out of its clutches. How can I remain silent at this supreme hour and hide my light under the bushel? Shall I ask the Japanese to tarry awhile? If today I sit quiet and inactive, God will take me to task for not using up the treasure He had given me, in the midst of the conflagration that is enveloping the whole world. Had the condition been different, I should have asked you to wait yet awhile. But the situation now has become intolerable, and the Congress has no other course left for it.

Nevertheless, the actual struggle does not commence this moment. You have only placed all your powers in my hands. I will now wait upon the Viceroy and plead with him for the acceptance of the Congress demand. That process is likely to take two or three weeks. What would you do in the meanwhile? What is the programme, for the interval, in which all can participate? As you know, the spinning wheel is the first thing that occurs to me. I made the same answer to the Maulana. He would have none of it, though he understood its import later. The fourteen-fold constructive programme is, of course, there for you to carry out. What more should you do? I will tell you. Every one of you should, from this moment onwards, consider yourself a free man or woman, and act as if you are free and are no longer under the heel of this imperialism.

It is not a make-believe that I am suggesting to you. It is the very essence of freedom. The bond of the slave is snapped the moment he considers himself to be a free being. He will plainly tell the master: 'I was your bond slave till this moment, but I am a slave no longer. You may kill me if you like, but if you keep me alive, I wish to tell you that if you release me from the bondage, of your own accord, I will ask for nothing more from you. You used to feed and clothe me, though I could have provided food and clothing for myself by my labour. I hitherto depended on you instead of on God, for food and raiment. But God has now inspired me with an urge for freedom and I am today a free man, and will no longer depend on you.'

You may take it from me that I am not going to strike a bargain with the Viceroy for ministries and the like. I am not going to be satisfied with anything short of complete freedom. Maybe he will propose the abolition of salt tax, the drink evil, etc. But I will say, 'Nothing less than freedom.'

Here is a mantra, a short one, that I give you. You may imprint it on your hearts and let every breath of yours give expression to it. The mantra is: 'Do or Die'. We shall either free India or die in the attempt; we shall not live to see the perpetuation of our slavery. Every true Congressman or woman will join the struggle with an inflexible determination not to remain alive to see the country in bondage and slavery. Let that be your pledge. Keep jails out of your consideration. If the government keep me free, I will not put on the government the strain of maintaining a large number of prisoners at a time, when it is in trouble. Let every man and woman live every moment of his or her life hereafter in the consciousness that he or she eats or lives for achieving freedom and will die, if need be, to attain that goal. Take a pledge, with God and your own conscience as witness, that you will no longer rest till freedom is achieved and will be prepared to lay down your lives in the attempt to achieve it. He who loses his life will gain it; he who will seek to save it shall lose it. Freedom is not for the coward or the faint-hearted.

A word to the journalists. I congratulate you on the support you have hitherto given to the national demand. I know the restrictions and handicaps under which you have to labour. But I would now ask you to snap the chains that bind you. It should be the proud privilege of the newspapers to lead and set an example in laying down one's life for freedom.

You have the pen which the government can't suppress. I know you have large properties in the form of printing presses, etc., and you would be afraid lest the government should attach them. I do not ask you to invite an attachment of the printing press voluntarily. For myself, I would not suppress my pen, even if the press was to be attached. As you know, my press was attached in the past and returned later on. But I do not ask from you that final sacrifice. I suggest a middle way. You should now wind up your standing committee, and you may declare that you will give up the pen only when India has won her freedom. You may tell Sir Frederick Puckle that he can't except from you a command performance, that his press notes are full of untruth, and that you will refuse to publish them. You will openly declare that you are wholeheartedly with the Congress. If you do this, you will have changed the atmosphere before the fight actually begins.

From the princes I ask with all respect due to them a very small thing. I am a well-wisher of the princes. I was born in a State. My grandfather refused to salute with his right hand any prince other than his own. But he did not say to the prince, as I feel he ought to have said, that even his own master could not compel him, his minister, to act against his conscience. I have eaten the prince's salt and I would not be false to it. As a faithful servant, it is my duty to warn the princes that if they will act while I am still alive, the princes may come to occupy an honourable place in free India. In Jawaharlal's scheme of free India, no privileges or the privileged classes have a place. Jawaharlal considers all property to be State-owned. He wants planned economy. He wants to reconstruct India according to plan. He likes to fly; I do not. I have kept a place for the princes and the zamindars in India that I envisage. I would ask the princes in all humility to enjoy through renunciation. The princes may renounce ownership over their properties and become their trustees in the true sense of the term. I visualize God in the assemblage of people. The princes may say to their people, 'You are the owners and masters of the State and we are your servants.' I would ask the princes to become servants of the people and render to them an account of their own services. The empire too bestows power on the princes, but they should prefer to derive power from their own people; and if they want to indulge in some innocent pleasures, they may seek to do so as servants of the people. I do not want the princes to live as paupers. But I would ask them, 'Do you want to remain slaves for all time? Why should you, instead of paying homage to a foreign power, not accept the sovereignty of your own people?' You may write to the Political Department, 'The people are now awake. How are we to withstand an avalanche before which even the large empires are crumbling? We, therefore, shall belong to the people from today onwards. We shall sink or swim with them.' Believe me, there is nothing unconstitutional in the course I am suggesting. There are, so far as I know, no treaties enabling the empire to coerce the princes. The people of the states will also declare that though they are the princes' subjects, they are part of the Indian nation and that they will accept the leadership of the princes, if the latter cast their lot with the people, but not otherwise. If this declaration enrages the princes and they choose to kill the people, the latter will meet death bravely and unflinchingly, but will not go back on their word.

Nothing, however, should be done secretly. This is an open rebellion. In this struggle secrecy is a sin. A free man would not engage in a secret movement. It is likely that when you gain freedom you will have a C.I.D. of your own, in spite of my advice to the contrary. But in the present struggle, we have to work openly and to receive bullets on our chest, without taking to heels.

I have a word to say to government servants also. They may not, if they like, resign their posts yet. The late Justice Ranade did not resign his post, but he openly declared that he belonged to the Congress. He said to the government that though he was a judge, he was a Congressman and would openly attend the sessions of the Congress, but that at the same time he would not let his political views warp his impartiality on the bench. He held Social Reform Conference in the very Pandal of the Congress. I would ask all the government servants to follow in the footsteps of Ranade and to declare their allegiance to the Congress as an answer to the secret circular issued by Sir Frederick Puckle.

This is all that I ask of you just now. I will now write to the Viceroy. You will be able to read the correspondence not just now but when I publish it with the Viceroy's consent.

But you are free to aver that you support the demand to be put forth in my letter. A judge came to me and said, 'We get secret circulars from high quarters. What are we to do?' I replied, 'If I were in your place, I would ignore the circulars.' You may openly say to the government, 'I have received your secret circular. I am, however, with the Congress. Though I serve the government for my livelihood, I am not going to obey these secret circulars or to employ underhand methods.'

Soldiers too are covered by the present programme. I do not ask them just now to resign their posts and to leave the army. The soldiers come to me, Jawaharlal and the Maulana and say, 'We are wholly with you. We are tired of the governmental tyranny.' To these soldiers I would say, 'You may say to the government, "Our hearts are with the Congress. We are not going to leave our posts. We will serve you so long as we receive your salaries. We will obey your just orders, but will refuse to fire on our own people."'

To those who lack the courage to do this much I have nothing to say. They will go their own way. But if you can do this much, you may take it from me that the whole atmosphere will be electrified. Let the government then shower bombs, if they like. But no power on earth will then be able to keep you in bondage any longer.

If the students want to join the struggle only to go back to their studies after a while, I would not invite them to it. For the present, however, till the time that I frame a programme for the struggle, I would ask the students to say to their professors, 'We belong to the Congress. Do you belong to the Congress, or to the government? If you belong to the Congress, you need not vacate your posts. You will remain at your posts but teach us and lead us unto freedom.' In all fights for freedom, the world over, the students have made very large contributions.

If in the interval that is left to us before the actual fight begins, you do even the little I have suggested to you, you will have changed the atmosphere and will have prepared the ground for the next step.

There is much I should yet like to say. But my heart is heavy. I have already taken up much of your time. I have yet to say a few words in English also. I thank you for the patience and attention with which you have listened to me even at this late hour. It is just what true soldiers would do. For the last twenty-two years, I have controlled my speech and pen and have stored up my energy. He is a true Brahmachari who does not fritter away his energy. He will, therefore, always control his speech. That has been my conscious effort all these years. But today the occasion has come when I had to unburden my heart before you. I have done so, even though it meant putting a strain on your patience; and I do not regret having done it. I have given you my message and through you I have delivered it to the whole of India.

III

I have taken such an inordinately long time over pouring out what was agitating my soul, to those whom I had just now the privilege of serving. I have been called their leader or, in the military language, their commander. But I do not look at my position in that light. I have no weapon but love to wield my authority over any one. I do sport a stick which you can break into bits without the slightest exertion. It is simply my staff with the help of which I walk. Such a cripple is not elated, when he has been called upon to bear the greatest burden. You can share that burden only when I appear before you not as your commander but as a humble servant. And he who serves best is the chief among equals.

Therefore, I was bound to share with you such thoughts as were welling up in my breast and tell you, in as summary a manner as I can, what I except you to do as the first step.

Let me tell you at the outset that the real struggle does not commence today. I have yet to go through much ceremonial as I always do. The burden, I confess, would be almost unbearable. I have to continue to reason in those circles with whom I have lost my credit and who have no trust left in me. I know that in the course of the last few weeks I have forfeited my credit with a large number of friends, so much so, that they have begun to doubt not only my wisdom but even my honesty. Now I hold my wisdom is not such a treasure which I cannot afford to lose; but my honesty is a precious treasure to me and I can ill-afford to lose it. I seem however to have lost it for the time being.

Friend of the Empire

Such occasions arise in the life of the man who is a pure seeker after truth and who would seek to serve the humanity and his country to the best of his lights without fear or hypocrisy. For the last fifty years I have known no other way. I have been a humble servant of humanity and have rendered on more than one occasion such services as I could to the Empire, and here let me say without fear of challenge that throughout my career never have I asked for any personal favour. I have enjoyed the privilege of friendship as I enjoy it today with Lord Linlithgow. It is a friendship which has outgrown official relationship. Whether Lord Linlithgow will bear me out, I do not know, but there is a personal bond between him and myself. He once introduced me to his daughter. His son-in-law, the A.D.C. was drawn towards me. He fell in love with Mahadev more than with me and Lady Anna and he came to me. She is an obedient and favourite daughter. I take interest in their welfare. I take the liberty to give out these personal and sacred titbits only to give you an earnest of the personal bond which exists between us and yet let me declare here that the personal bond will never interfere with the stubborn struggle on which, if it falls to my lot, I may have to launch against Lord Linlithgow, as the representative of the Empire. I will have to resist the might of that Empire with the might of the dumb millions with no limit but of non-violence as policy confined to this struggle. It is a terrible job to have to offer resistance to a Viceroy with whom I enjoy such relations. He has more than once trusted my word, often about my people. I would love to repeat that experiment, as it stands to his credit. I mention this with great pride and pleasure. I mention it as an earnest of my desire to be true to the Empire when that Empire forfeited my trust and the Englishman who was its Viceroy came to know it.

Charlie Andrews

Then there is the sacred memory of Charlie Andrews which wells up within me. At this moment the spirit of Andrews hovers about me. For me he sums up the brightest traditions of English culture. I enjoyed closer relations with him than with most Indians. I enjoyed his confidence. There were no secrets between us. We exchanged our hearts every day. Whatever was in his heart, he would blurt out without the slightest hesitation or reservation. It is true he was a friend of Gurudev* but he looked upon Gurudev with awe. He had that peculiar humility. But with me he became the closest friend. Years ago he came to me with a note of introduction from Gokhale. Pearson and he were the first-rank specimens of Englishmen. I know that his spirit is listening to me.

Then I have got a warm letter of congratulations from the Metropolitan of Calcutta. I hold him to be a man of God. Today he is opposed to me.

---

*Rabindranath Tagore

Voice of Conscience

With all this background, I want to declare to the world, although I may have forfeited the regard of many friends in the West and I must bow my head low; but even for their friendship or love I must not suppress the voice of conscience—promoting of my inner basic nature today. There is something within me impelling me to cry out my agony. I have known humanity. I have studied something of psychology. Such a man knows exactly what it is. I do not mind how you describe it. That voice within tells me, 'You have to stand against the whole world although you may have to stand alone. You have to stare in the face the whole world although the world may look at you with bloodshot eyes. Do not fear. Trust the little voice residing within your heart.' It says, 'Forsake friends, wife and all; but testify to that for which you have lived and for which you have to die.' I want to live my full span of life. And for me I put my span of life at 120 years. By that time India will be free, the world will be free.

Real Freedom

Let me tell you that I do not regard England or for that matter America as free countries. They are free after their own fashion, free to hold in bondage coloured races of the earth. Are England and America fighting for the liberty of these races today? If not, do not ask me to wait until after the war. You shall not limit my concept of freedom. The English and American teachers, their history, their magnificent poetry have not said that you shall not broaden the interpretation of freedom. And according to my interpretation of that freedom I am constrained to say they are strangers to that freedom which their teachers and poets have described. If they will know the real freedom they should come to India. They have to come not with pride or arrogances but in the spite of real earnest seekers of truth. It is a fundamental truth which India has been experimenting with for 22 years.

Congress and Non-violence

Unconsciously from its very foundations long ago the Congress has been building on non-violence known as constitutional methods. Dadabhai and Pherozeshah who had held the Congress India in the palm of their hands became rebels. They were lovers of the Congress. They were its masters. But above all they were real servants. They never countenanced murder, secrecy and the like. I confess there are many black sheep amongst us Congressmen. But I trust the whole of India today to launch upon a non-violent struggle. I trust because of my nature to rely upon the innate goodness of human nature which perceives the truth and prevails during the crisis as if by instinct. But even if I am deceived in this I shall not swerve. I shall not flinch. From its very inception the Congress based its policy on peaceful methods, included Swaraj and the subsequent generations added non-violence. When Dadabhai entered the British Parliament, Salisbury dubbed him as a black man; but the English people defeated Salisbury and Dadabhai went to the Parliament by their vote. India was delirious with joy. These things however India has outgrown.

I will Go Ahead

It is, however, with all these things as the background that I want Englishmen, Europeans and all the United Nations to examine in their hearts what crime India had committed in demanding Independence. I ask, is it right for you to distrust such an organization with all its background, tradition and record of over half a century and misrepresent its endeavours before all the world by every means at your command? Is it right that by hook or by crook, aided by the foreign press, aided by the President of the U.S.A., or even by the Generalissimo of China who has yet to win his laurels, you should present India's struggle in shocking caricature? I have met the Generalissimo. I have known him through Madame Shek who was my interpreter; and though he seemed inscrutable to me, not so Madame Shek; and he allowed me to read his mind through her. There is a chorus of disapproval and righteous protest all over the world against us. They say we are erring, the move is inopportune. I had great regard for British diplomacy which has enabled them to hold the Empire so long. Now it stinks in my nostrils, and others have studied that diplomacy and are putting it into practice. They may succeed in getting, through these methods, world opinion on their side for a time; but India will speak against that world opinion. She will raise her voice against all the organized propaganda. I will speak against it. Even if all the United Nations opposed me, even if the whole of India forsakes me, I will say, 'You are wrong. India will wrench with non-violence her liberty from unwilling hands.' I will go ahead not for India's sake alone, but for the sake of the world. Even if my eyes close before there is freedom, non-violence will not end. They will be dealing a mortal blow to China and to Russia if they oppose the freedom of non-violent India which is pleading with bended knees for the fulfilment of debt long overdue. Does a creditor ever go to the debtor like that? And even when India is met with such angry opposition, she says, 'We won't hit below the belt, we have learnt sufficient gentlemanliness. We are pledged to non-violence.' I have been the author of non-embarrassment policy of the Congress and yet today you find me talking this strong language. I say it is consistent with our honour. If a man holds me by the neck and wants to drown me, may I not struggle to free myself directly? There is no inconsistency in our position today.

Appeal to the United Nations

There are representatives of the foreign press assembled here today. Through them I wish to say to the world that the

United Powers who somehow or other say that they have need for India, have the opportunity now to declare India free and prove their bona fides. If they miss it, they will be missing the opportunity of their lifetime, and history will record that they did not discharge their obligations to India in time, and lost the battle. I want the blessings of the whole world so that I may succeed with them. I do not want the United Powers to go beyond their obvious limitations. I do not want them to accept non-violence and disarm today. There is a fundamental difference between fascism and this imperialism which I am fighting. Do the British get from India all they want? What they get today is from India which they hold in bondage. Think what difference it would make if India was to participate as a free ally. That freedom, if it is to come, must come today. It will have no taste left in it if today you who have the power to help cannot exercise it. If you can exercise it, under the glow of freedom what seems impossible, today, will become possible tomorrow. If India feels that freedom, she will command that freedom for China. The road for running to Russia's help will be open. The Englishmen did not die in Malaya or on Burma soil. What shall enable us to retrieve the situation? Where shall I go, and where shall I take the forty crores of India? How is this vast mass of humanity to be aglow in the cause of world deliverance, unless and until it has touched and felt freedom. Today they have no touch of life left. It has been crushed out of them. If lustre is to be put into their eyes, freedom has to come not tomorrow, but today.

Gandhi speaks at the prayer meeting.

Kashmir Issue

Gandhi Sevagram Ashram, Wardha
4 January 1948

Today there is talk of war everywhere. Everyone fears a war breaking out between the two countries. If that happens it will be a calamity both for India and for Pakistan. India has written to the U.N. because whenever there is a fear of conflict anywhere the U.N. is asked to promote a settlement and to stop fighting from breaking out. India therefore wrote to the U.N.O. However trivial the issue may appear to be, it could lead to a war between the two countries. It is a long memorandum and it has been cabled. Pakistan's leaders Zafrullah Khan and Liaquat Ali Khan have since issued long statements. I would take leave to say that their argument does not appeal to me. You may ask if I approve of the Union government approaching the U.N.O. I may say that I both approve and do not approve of what they did. I approve of it because after all what else are they to do? They are convinced that what they are doing is right. If there are raids from outside the frontier of Kashmir, the obvious conclusion is that it must be with the connivance of Pakistan. Pakistan can deny it. But the denial does not settle the matter. Kashmir has acceded the accession upon certain conditions. If Pakistan harasses Kashmir and if Sheikh Abdullah who is the leader of Kashmir asks the Indian Union for help, the latter is bound to send help. Such help therefore was sent to Kashmir. At the same time Pakistan is being requested to get out of Kashmir and to arrive at a settlement with India over the question through bilateral negotiations. If no settlement can be reached in this way then a war is inevitable. It is to avoid the possibility of war that the Union government has taken the step it did. Whether they are right in doing so or not God alone knows. Whatever might have been the attitude of Pakistan, if I had my way I would have invited Pakistan's representatives to India and we could have met, discussed the matter and worked out some settlement. They keep saying that they want an amicable settlement but they do nothing to create the conditions for such a settlement. I shall therefore humbly say to the responsible leaders of Pakistan that though we are now two countries—which is a thing I never wanted—we should at least try to arrive at an agreement so that we could live as peaceful neighbours. Let us grant for the sake of argument that all Indians are bad, but Pakistan at least is a newborn nation which has moreover come into being in the name of religion and it should at least keep itself clean. But they themselves make no such claim. It is not their argument that Muslims have committed no atrocities in Pakistan. I shall therefore suggest that it is now their duty, as far as possible, to arrive at an amicable understanding with India and live in harmony with her. Mistakes were made on both sides. Of this I have no doubt. But this does not mean that we should persist in those mistakes, for then in the end we shall only destroy ourselves in a war and the whole of the subcontinent will pass into the hands of some third power. That will be the worst imaginable fate for us. I shudder to think of it. Therefore the two dominions should come together with God as witness and find a settlement. The matter is now before the U.N.O. It cannot be withdrawn from there. But if India and Pakistan come to a settlement the big powers in the U.N.O. will have to endorse that settlement. They will not object to the settlement. They themselves can only say that they will do their best to see that the two countries arrive at an understanding through mutual discussions. Let us pray to God to grant that we may either learn to live in amity with each other or if we must fight, to let us fight to the very end. That may be folly but sooner or later it will purify us. Now a few words about Delhi. I came to know of the incidents which took place last evening through Brijkishan. I had gone to the Camp for the evening prayer. I came away after the prayer but he had stayed over to talk to the people in the Camp. There are some Muslim houses at a little distance from the Camp. About four or five hundred inmates of the Camp mostly women and children but also some men issued out of the Camp to take possession of the houses. I am told they did not indulge in any kind of violence. Some of the houses were vacant. Some were occupied by the owners. They tried to take possession even of the latter. The police were near at hand. They immediately went to the spot and brought the situation under control at about 9 o'clock according to the information I have. The police have stayed on there. I understand they had to use tear gas. Tear gas does not kill but it can be pretty painful. I am told that something has happened today again.

All I can say is that is a matter of great shame for us. Have not the refugees learnt even from their immense suffering that they have to exercise some restraint? It is highly improper to go and occupy other people's houses. It is for the government to find them shelter or whatever else their need. Today the government is our own. But if we defy our own government and defy the police and forcibly occupy houses the government is not likely to continue for long. It is still worse that such things should happen in the capital city of India where there are so many ambassadors from all over the world. Do we want to show them the spectacle of people occupying whatever they can? It is all the more regrettable that women and children were used as a shield. It is inhuman. It is like Muslim rulers keeping a herd of cows in the vanguard of their armies to make sure that the Hindus would not fight. It is uncivilized, barbaric behaviour. It is still more barbaric to put women and children in front to provide against the police making a lathi charge. It is abuse of womanhood. I must humbly ask all the refugees—women and children—not to behave in this way. Let them settle down. If they don't, then apart from a war between India and Pakistan, we may kill ourselves in mutual strife. We may lose Delhi and make ourselves the laughing-stock of the world. If we want to keep India a free country, we must stop the things that are at present going on.

9

Napoleon Bonaparte

*'The patience and courage you have shown in the midst of
these rocks are admirable; but they gain you no renown;
no glory results to you from your endurance.'*

∿

*The campaign fought by the French General in Italy in
1796-97 helped end the French Revolutionary Wars,
marking a victory for France. Napoleon proved that
he was not just a great leader on the battlefield but a
remarkable orator as well.*

**Napoleon's Address to the Army at the Beginning of the
Italian Campaign**

Northern Italy
March 1796

'Soldiers, you are naked and ill-fed! Government owes you

much and can give you nothing. The patience and courage you have shown in the midst of these rocks are admirable; but they gain you no renown; no glory results to you from your endurance. It is my design to lead you into the most fertile plains of the world. Rich provinces and great cities will be in your power; there you will find honour, glory and wealth. Soldiers of Italy! Will you be wanting in courage or perseverance?'

◆

This speech by Napoleon echoes the accomplishments of the commanding general and his army.

Napoleon's Proclamation to the Army, May 1796

Italy
May 1796

'Soldiers, you have in fifteen days won six victories, taken twenty-one stand of colours, fifty-five pieces of cannon, and several fortresses, and overrun the richest part of Piedmont; you have made 15,000 prisoners, and killed or wounded upwards of 10,000 men. Hitherto you have been fighting for barren rocks, made memorable by your valour, though useless to your country, but your exploits now equal those of the armies of Holland and the Rhine. You were utterly destitute, and you have supplied all your wants. You have gained battles without cannon, passed rivers without bridges, performed forced marches without shoes, and bivouacked without strong liquors, and often without bread. None but Republican phalanxes, the soldiers of liberty, could have endured what you have done; thanks to you, soldiers, for your perseverance! Your grateful country owes its safety to you; and if the taking of Toulon was an earnest of the immortal campaign of 1794, your present victories foretell one more glorious. The two armies which lately attacked you in full confidence now fly before you in consternation; the perverse men who laughed at your distress, and inwardly rejoiced at the triumph of your enemies, are now confounded and trembling. But, soldiers, you have yet done nothing, for there still remains much to do. Neither Turin nor Milan are yours; the ashes of the conquerors of Tarquin are still trodden underfoot by the assassins of Basseville.* It is said that there are some among you whose courage is shaken, and who would prefer returning to the summits of the Alps and Apennines. No, I cannot believe it. The victors of Montenotte, Millesimo, Dego and Mondovi are eager to extend the glory of the French name!'

◆

---

*Nicolas-Jean-Hugon de Basseville (1753–1793) was a French diplomat killed by a Roman mob on January 13, 1793.

*Bonaparte said that it was Lodi that made him certain
he could be a man of high destiny.*

Letter to 'The Directory'

Headquarters, Lodi
11 May 1796

Citizen Directors, I thought that the passage of the Po would
be the most audacious performance of the campaign, the
Battle of Millesimo the liveliest encounter, but I have yet
to give you an account of the Battle of Lodi.

At three o'clock on the morning of the 21st, we pitched
our headquarters at Casal. At nine o'clock, our vanguard
encountered the enemy defending the approaches to Lodi.
I immediately ordered all the cavalry to mount with four
pieces of light artillery, which had just arrived, drawn by
the carriage horses of the lords of Plaisance.

The division of General Augereau, which had camped
overnight at Borghetto, and that of General Masséna, which
slept at Casal, were put in motion. Meantime, our vanguard
had overturned all the posts of the enemy, and seized one
of their cannon. We pursued the enemy into Lodi; they
having already crossed the Adda by the bridge. Beaulieu,
with all his army, was drawn up in battle array. Thirty set
cannon defended the passage of the bridge. I formed all
my artillery into a battery. The cannonading was very lively
for several hours.

As soon as the army arrived, it formed into a close

column with the second battalion of rifles at its head, followed by all the battalions of grenadiers. On the run, with cries of *Vive la République*, they appeared on the bridge, which is over six-hundred-feet long. The enemy kept up a terrible fire. The head of the column almost seemed to waver. A moment's hesitation and all would have been lost. The Generals Berthier, Masséna, Cervoni, Dallemagne, the Brigadier-General Lannes, the Battalion-Commander Dupas felt this, and rushing to the front, decided the fate of the day.

This redoubtable column overrode all opposition, breaking Beaulieu's order of battle, capturing all his artillery, and sowing on all sides, seeds of terror, flight and death. In the twinkling of an eye, the enemy's army was dispersed. The Generals Rusca, Augereau and Beyrand crossed as soon as their divisions arrived, and completed the victory. The cavalry crossed the Adda at a ford; but the ford proving extremely bad, there was much delay, which prevented an engagement.

The enemy's cavalry tried charging our troops, in order to protect the retreat of their infantry, but our men were hard to frighten.

Nightfall and the extreme fatigue of the troops, many of whom had made more than ten leagues during the day, forced us to forego the pleasure of pursuit.

The enemy lost twenty pieces of cannon, and from two to three thousand killed, wounded or prisoners. We lost but 150 men, dead and wounded.

Citizen Latour, General Masséna's captain aide-de-camp, received several sabre cuts. I want the place of battalion commander for this brave officer.

Citizen Marmont, my aide-de-camp brigadier-general, had a horse shot under him.

Citizen Lemarois, my captain aide-de-camp, had his clothes riddled by balls. The courage of this young officer is equal to his activity.

If called upon to name all the soldiers who distinguished themselves on that extraordinary day, I should be obliged to name all the riflemen and grenadiers of the vanguard, and nearly all the officers of the staff. But I must not forget the intrepid Berthier, who was, in one day, gunner, cavalier, and grenadier. Brigadier-General Sugny, commanding the artillery, conducted himself creditably.

Beaulieu fled with the remains of his army. Already Normandy may be considered as belonging to the Republic. At this moment, Beaulieu is passing through the Venetian States, many of whose cities have closed their doors upon him.

I hope soon to send you the keys of Milan and Pavia.

Although, since the beginning of the campaign, we have had some pretty hot encounters, which the army of the French Republic have met with audacity, not one of them has approached the terrible passage of the bridge at Lodi.

If we have lost but few good men, it is due to promptness of execution, and to the sudden effect produced upon the opposing army by the size and formidable fire of our intrepid column.

◆

The Battle of Lodi cemented Bonaparte's relationship with his troops, who admired him for his courage and bravery and willingness to face dangers as they were doing.

Letter to 'The Directory'

Headquarters, Lodi
14 May 1796

Citizen Directors, I think it most impolitic to divide the Italian army into two sections; it is equally contrary to the interests of the Republic to put two generals in command.

The expedition against Livourne, Rome and Naples is a small affair; it can be accomplished by arranging the divisions in echelon in such a manner as to enable them, by a retrograde march, to appear in force against the Austrians, and threaten to hem them in at the slightest movement on their part.

For this, it is not only necessary to have *one* general, but he should have nothing to hinder him in his march or in his operations. I have conducted the campaign without consulting anyone. I should have accomplished nothing worth the trouble had I been obliged to reconcile my ideas with those of another. I have gained some advantages over very superior forces while in an almost destitute condition;

because I was persuaded of your entire confidence in me, my moves were as prompt as my thoughts.

If you fetter me on all sides; if it is necessary for me to confer with the commissioners of the government regarding each step; if they have the right to change my movements, to send me troops or withdraw them at their will, then look for no good.

If you reduce your power by dividing your forces, if you break the unity of the military outline in Italy, with grief I tell you, you will have lost the most favourable occasion for bringing Italy to terms.

In the present condition of the affairs of the Republic in Italy, it is indispensable for you to have a general in whom you have entire confidence. If it is not I, I make no complaint, I shall only strive to redouble my zeal in order to merit your esteem in the past that you may confide in me. Everyone has his own manner of conducting war. General Kellerman has had more experience and will do better than I, but together we would make a dire failure.

I cannot render our country any essential service unless invested with your absolute and entire confidence. It requires much courage on my part to write you in this way, I could so easily be accused of pride and ambition. But I owe the expression of all my opinions on the subject to one whose many tokens of esteem I shall never forget.

◆

Napoleon inspires confidence in the French soldiers.

Proclamation to the Soldiers on Entering Milan

Italy
15 May 1796

Soldiers, you have rushed like a torrent from the top of the Apennines; you have overthrown and scattered all that opposed your march. Piedmont, delivered from Austrian tyranny, indulges her natural sentiments of peace and friendship toward France. Milan is yours, and the Republican flag waves throughout Lombardy. The Dukes of Parma and Modena owe their political existence to your generosity alone. The army, which so proudly threatened you, can find no barrier to protect it against your courage; neither the Po, the Ticino, nor the Adda could stop you for a single day. These vaunted bulwarks of Italy opposed you in vain; you passed them as rapidly as the Apennines. These great successes have filled the heart of your country with joy. Your representatives have ordered a festival to commemorate your victories, which has been held in every district of the Republic. There your fathers, your wives, sisters and mistresses rejoiced in your good fortune and proudly boasted of belonging to you. Yes, soldiers, you have done much—but remains there nothing more to do? Shall it be said of us that we have conquered, but not now to make use of victory? Shall posterity reproach us with having found

Capau in Lombardy? But I see you already hasten to arms. An effeminate response is tedious to you; the days which are lost to glory are lost to your happiness. Well, then, let us set forth! We have still forced marches to make, enemies to subdue, laurels to gather, injuries to revenge. Let those who have sharpened the daggers of civil war in France, who have basely murdered our ministers, and burnt our ships at Toulon, tremble! The hour of vengeance has struck; but let the people of all countries be free from apprehension; we are the friends of the people everywhere, and those great men whom we have taken for our models. To restore the capitol, to replace the statues of the heroes who rendered it illustrious, to rouse the Roman people, stupefied by several ages of slavery—such will be the fruit of our victories; they will form an era for posterity, you will have the immortal glory of changing the face of the finest part of Europe. The French people, free and respected by the whole world, will give to Europe a glorious peace, which will indemnify them for the sacrifices of every kind, which for last six years they have been making. You will then return to your homes and your country. Men will say, as they point you out, 'He belonged to the army of Italy.'

◆

Napoleon reminds his soldiers of the ancient friendship they shared with the Republic of Venice whom they are entering.

Proclamation to the Troops on Entering Brescia

Italy
28 May 1796

It is to deliver the finest country in Europe from the iron yoke of the proud House of Austria, that the French army has braved the most formidable obstacles. Victory, siding with justice, has crowned its efforts with success, the wreck of the enemy's army has retreated behind the Mincio. In order to pursue them, the French army enters the territory of the Republic of Venice; but it will not forget that the two Republics are united by ancient friendship. Religion, government and customs shall be respected. Let the people be free from apprehension, the severest discipline will be kept up; whatever the army is supplied with shall be punctually paid for in money. The general-in-chief invites the officers of the Republic of Venice, the magistrates and priests to make known his sentiments to the people, in order that the friendship which has so long subsisted between the two nations may be cemented by confidence. Faithful in the path of honour as in that of victory, the French soldier is terrible only to the enemies of his liberty and his government.

◆

Napoleon rebukes soldiers of a few regiments who lack courage.

Address to the Soldiers during the Siege of Mantua

Italy
6 November 1796

Soldiers, I am not satisfied with you; you have shown neither bravery, discipline, nor perseverance; no position could rally you; you abandoned yourselves to a panic-terror; you suffered yourselves to be driven from situations where a handful of brave men might have stopped an army. Soldiers of the 39th and 85th, you are not French soldiers. Quartermaster-general, let it be inscribed on their colours, 'They no longer form part of the Army of Italy!'

◆

Napoleon praises his soldiers who have fought valiantly.

Address to the Troops on the Conclusion of the First Italian Campaign

Italy
March 1797

Soldiers, the campaign just ended has given you imperishable renown. You have been victorious in fourteen pitched battles and seventy actions. You have taken more than a hundred thousand prisoners, five hundred field-pieces, two thousand heavy guns, and four pontoon trains. You have maintained the army during the whole campaign. In addition to this, you have sent six millions of dollars to the public treasury, and have enriched the National Museum with three hundred masterpieces of the arts of ancient and modern Italy, which it has required thirty centuries to produce. You have conquered the finest countries in Europe. The French flag waves for the first time upon the Adriatic opposite to Macedon, the native country of Alexander (the Great). Still higher destinies await you. I know that you will not prove unworthy of them. Of all the foes that conspired to stifle the Republic in its birth, the Austrian Emperor alone remains before you. To obtain peace, we must seek it in the heart of his hereditary State. You will there find a brave people, whose religion and customs you will respect, and whose prosperity you will hold sacred. Remember that it is liberty you carry to the brave Hungarian nation.

◆

Napoleon asks the people of Genoa to be civil and not afraid and hostile.

Address to the Genoese

Italy
1797

I will respond, citizens, to the confidence you have reposed in me. It is not enough that you refrain from hostility to religion. You should do nothing which can cause inquietude to tender consciences. To exclude the nobles from any public office is an act of extreme injustice. You thus repeat the wrong which you condemn in them. Why are you people of Genoa so changed? Their first impulses of fraternal kindness have been succeeded by terror and fear. Remember that the priests were the first who rallied around the tree of liberty. They first told you that the morality of the gospel is democratic. Men have taken advantage of the faults, perhaps the crimes of individual priests, to unite against Christianity. You have proscribed without discrimination. When a State becomes accustomed to condemn without hearing, to applaud a discourse because it is impassioned; when exaggeration and madness are called virtue, moderation and equity designated as crimes, that State is near its ruin. Believe me, I shall consider that one of the happiest moments of my life in which I hear that the people of Genoa are united among themselves and live happily.

◆

Napoleon talks about his plans for expansion.

Extract from a Letter to the Directory

Italy
April 1797

From these different posts, we shall command the Mediterranean, we shall keep an eye on the Ottoman

Empire, which is crumbling to pieces, and we shall have it in our power to render the dominion of the ocean almost useless to the English. They have possession of the Cape of Good Hope. We can do without it. Let us occupy Egypt. We shall be in the direct road for India. It will be easy for us to found there one of the finest colonies in the world. It is in Egypt that we must attack England.

◆

Napoleon boosts the morale of his soldiers before setting out for Germany.

Address to Soldiers after the Signing of the Treaty of Campo Formio

Italy
October 1797

Soldiers, I set out tomorrow for Germany. Separated from the army, I shall sigh for the moment of my rejoining it, and brave fresh dangers. Whatever post government may assign to the soldiers of the Army of Italy, they will always be the worthy supporters of liberty and of the glory of the French name. Soldiers, when you talk of the Princes you have conquered, of the nations you have set free, and the battles you have fought in two campaigns, say, in the next two, we shall do still more!

◆

Napoleon speaks like a true general, telling people how to build their true destiny.

Proclamation to the Cisalpine Republic

Italy
17 November 1797

We have given you liberty. Take care you preserve it. To be worthy of your destiny, make only discreet and honourable laws, and cause them to be executed with energy. Favour the diffusion of knowledge, and respect religion. Compose your battalions not of disreputable men, but with citizens imbued with the principles of the Republic, and closely linked with the prosperity. You have need to impress yourselves with the feelings of your strength, and with the dignity which befits the free man. Divided and bowed by ages of tyranny, you could not alone have achieved your independence. In a few years, if true to yourselves, no nation will be strong enough to wrest liberty from you. Till then, the great nation will protect you.

◆

Napoleon shares his vision with the people about the freedom of the whole of Europe.

Address to the Citizens after the Signing of the Treaty of Camp Formio

Italy
10 December 1797

Citizens, the French people, in order to be free, had kings to combat. To obtain a constitution founded on reason, it had the prejudices of eighteen centuries to overcome. Priestcraft, feudalism, despotism, have successively, for two thousand years, governed Europe. From the peace you have just concluded dates the era of representative governments. You have succeeded in organizing the great nation, whose vast territory is circumscribed only because nature herself has fixed its limits. You have done more. The two finest countries in Europe, formerly as renowned for the arts, the sciences, and the illustrious men, whose cradle they were, see with the greatest hopes genius and freedom issuing from the tomb of their ancestors. I have the honour to deliver to you the treaty signed at Camp Formio, and ratified by the Emperor. Peace secures the liberty, the prosperity, and the glory of the Republic. As soon as the happiness of France is secured by the best organic laws, the whole of Europe will be free.

◆

*A truly dramatic moment in history occurred on 20 April
1814, as Napoleon Bonaparte, Emperor of France and*

would-be ruler of Europe, said goodbye to the Old Guard
after his failed invasion of Russia and defeat by the Allies.

Farewell to the Old Guard following the Failed Invasion of Russia and Defeat by the Allies

Fontenbleu, France
1814

Soldiers of my Old Guard, I bid you farewell. For twenty years, I have constantly accompanied you on the road to honour and glory. In these latter times, as in the days of our prosperity, you have invariably been models of courage and fidelity. With men such as you, our cause could not be lost; but the war would have been interminable; it would have been civil war, and that would have entailed deeper misfortunes on France.

I have sacrificed all of my interests to those of the country.

I go; but you, my friends, will continue to serve France.

10

Nelson Mandela

*'The need to unite the people of our country is as
important a task now as it always has been.'*

∿

*On 11 February 1990, Nelson Mandela, after more than
a quarter of a century behind bars, walked through
the gates of Victor Verster Prison. Later, he addressed
the nation at a huge rally in Cape Town. The speech
was broadcast live around the world. He was declared
President of South Africa in Pretoria on 10 May 1994.*

Nelson Mandela's Speech on His Release from Prison*

Cape Town, South Africa
11 February 1990

Friends, comrades and fellow South Africans, I greet you

---

*Source: Nelson Mandela Foundation

all in the name of peace, democracy and freedom for all.

I stand here before you not as a prophet but as a humble servant of you, the people. Your tireless and heroic sacrifices have made it possible for me to be here today. I therefore place the remaining years of my life in your hands.

On this day of my release, I extend my sincere and warmest gratitude to the millions of my compatriots and those in every corner of the globe who have campaigned tirelessly for my release.

I send special greetings to the people of Cape Town, this city which has been my home for three decades. Your mass marches and other forms of struggle have served as a constant source of strength to all political prisoners.

I salute the African National Congress. It has fulfilled our every expectation in its role as leader of the great march to freedom.

I salute our President, Comrade Oliver Tambo, for leading the ANC even under the most difficult circumstances.

I salute the rank and file members of the ANC. You have sacrificed life and limb in the pursuit of the noble cause of our struggle.

I salute combatants of Umkhonto we Sizwe, like Solomon Mahlangu and Ashley Kriel who have paid the ultimate price for the freedom of all South Africans.

I salute the South African Communist Party for its sterling contribution to the struggle for democracy. You have survived forty years of unrelenting persecution. The memory of great communists like Moses Kotane, Yusuf

Dadoo, Bram Fischer and Moses Mabhida will be cherished for generations to come.

I salute General Secretary Joe Slovo, one of our finest patriots. We are heartened by the fact that the alliance between ourselves and the Party remains as strong as it always was.

I salute the United Democratic Front, the National Education Crisis Committee, the South African Youth Congress, the Transvaal and Natal Indian Congresses and COSATU and the many other formations of the Mass Democratic Movement.

I also salute the Black Sash and the National Union of South African Students. We note with pride that you have acted as the conscience of white South Africa. Even during the darkest days in the history of our struggle you held the flag of liberty high. The large scale mass mobilization of the past few years is one of the key factors which led to the opening of the final chapter of our struggle.

I extend my greetings to the working class of our country. Your organized strength is the pride of our movement. You remain the most dependable force in the struggle to end exploitation and oppression.

I pay tribute to the many religious communities who carried the campaign for justice forward when the organizations for our people were silenced.

I greet the traditional leaders of our country—many of you continue to walk in the footsteps of great heroes like Hintsa and Sekhukune.

I pay tribute to the endless heroism of youth, you, the

young lions. You, the young lions, have energized our entire struggle.

I pay tribute to the mothers and wives and sisters of our nation. You are the rock-hard foundation of our struggle. Apartheid has inflicted more pain on you than on anyone else.

On this occasion, we thank the world community for their great contribution to the anti-apartheid struggle. Without your support our struggle would not have reached this advanced stage. The sacrifice of the frontline states will be remembered by South Africans forever.

My salutations would be incomplete without expressing my deep appreciation for the strength given to me during my long and lonely years in prison by my beloved wife and family. I am convinced that your pain and suffering was far greater than my own.

Before I go any further I wish to make the point that I intend making only a few preliminary comments at this stage. I will make a more complete statement only after I have had the opportunity to consult with my comrades.

Today, the majority of South Africans, black and white, recognize that apartheid has no future. It has to be ended by our own decisive mass action in order to build peace and security. The mass campaign of defiance and other actions of our organization and people can only culminate in the establishment of democracy. The destruction caused by apartheid on our subcontinent is incalculable. The fabric of family life of millions of my people has been shattered.

Millions are homeless and unemployed. Our economy lies in ruins and our people are embroiled in political strife. Our resort to the armed struggle in 1960 with the formation of the military wing of the ANC, Umkhonto we Sizwe, was a purely defensive action against the violence of apartheid. The factors which necessitated the armed struggle still exist today. We have no option but to continue. We express the hope that a climate conducive to a negotiated settlement will be created soon so that there may no longer be the need for the armed struggle.

I am a loyal and disciplined member of the African National Congress. I am, therefore, in full agreement with all of its objectives, strategies and tactics.

The need to unite the people of our country is as important a task now as it always has been. No individual leader is able to take on this enormous task on his own. It is our task as leaders to place our views before our organization and to allow the democratic structures to decide. On the question of democratic practice, I feel duty-bound to make the point that a leader of the movement is a person who has been democratically elected at a national conference. This is a principle which must be upheld without any exceptions.

Today, I wish to report to you that my talks with the government have been aimed at normalizing the political situation in the country. We have not as yet begun discussing the basic demands of the struggle. I wish to stress that I myself have at no time entered into negotiations about the future of our country except to insist on a meeting between the ANC and the government.

Mr De Klerk has gone further than any other Nationalist president in taking real steps to normalize the situation. However, there are further steps as outlined in the Harare Declaration that have to be met before negotiations on the basic demands of our people can begin. I reiterate our call for, inter alia, the immediate ending of the State of Emergency and the freeing of all, and not only some, political prisoners. Only such a normalized situation, which allows for free political activity, can allow us to consult our people in order to obtain a mandate.

The people need to be consulted on who will negotiate and on the content of such negotiations. Negotiations cannot take place above the heads or behind the backs of our people. It is our belief that the future of our country can only be determined by a body which is democratically elected on a non-racial basis. Negotiations on the dismantling of apartheid will have to address the overwhelming demand of our people for a democratic, non-racial and unitary South Africa. There must be an end to white monopoly on political power and a fundamental restructuring of our political and economic systems to ensure that the inequalities of apartheid are addressed and our society thoroughly democratized.

It must be added that Mr De Klerk himself is a man of integrity who is acutely aware of the dangers of a public figure not honouring his undertakings. But as an organization we base our policy and strategy on the harsh reality we are faced with. And this reality is that we are still suffering under the policy of the Nationalist government.

Our struggle has reached a decisive moment. We call on our people to seize this moment so that the process towards democracy is rapid and uninterrupted. We have waited too long for our freedom. We can no longer wait. Now is the time to intensify the struggle on all fronts. To relax our efforts now would be a mistake which generations to come will not be able to forgive. The sight of freedom looming on the horizon should encourage us to redouble our efforts.

It is only through disciplined mass action that our victory can be assured. We call on our white compatriots to join us in the shaping of a new South Africa. The freedom movement is a political home for you too. We call on the international community to continue the campaign to isolate the apartheid regime. To lift sanctions now would be to run the risk of aborting the process towards the complete eradication of apartheid.

Our march to freedom is irreversible. We must not allow fear to stand in our way.

Universal suffrage on a common voters' role in a united democratic and non-racial South Africa is the only way to peace and racial harmony.

In conclusion I wish to quote my own words during my trial in 1964. They are true today as they were then:

'I have fought against white domination and I have fought against black domination. I have cherished the ideal of a democratic and free society in which all persons live together in harmony and with equal opportunities. It is an ideal which I hope to live for and to achieve. But if need be, it is an ideal for which I am prepared to die.'

11

Woodrow Wilson

'No statesman who has the least conception of his responsibility ought for a moment to permit himself to continue this tragical and appalling outpouring of blood and treasure...'

ᔿ

In January 1918, some ten months before the end of World War I, President Woodrow Wilson appeared before a joint session of Congress and delivered this address suggesting possible peace terms to end the four-year-old European conflict. These suggestions are now historically known as Fourteen Points.

Fourteen Points

U.S. Congress, Washington, D.C.
8 January 1918

Gentlemen of the Congress, once more, as repeatedly before, the spokesmen of the Central Empires have indicated their desire to discuss the objects of the war and the possible basis of a general peace. Parleys have been in progress at Brest-Litovsk between Russian representatives and representatives of the Central Powers to which the attention of all the belligerents has been invited for the purpose of ascertaining whether it may be possible to extend these parleys into a general conference with regard to terms of peace and settlement.

The Russian representatives presented not only a perfectly definite statement of the principles upon which they would be willing to conclude peace, but also an equally definite programme of the concrete application of those principles. The representatives of the Central Powers, on their part, presented an outline of settlement which, if much less definite, seemed susceptible of liberal interpretation until their specific programme of practical terms was added. That programme proposed no concessions at all, either to the sovereignty of Russia or to the preferences of the populations with whose fortunes it dealt, but meant, in a word, that the Central Empires were to keep every foot of territory their armed forces had occupied—every province, every city, every point of vantage as a permanent addition to their territories and their power.

It is a reasonable conjecture that the general principles of settlement which they at first suggested originated with the more liberal statesmen of Germany and Austria, the men who have begun to feel the force of their own people's thought and purpose, while the concrete terms of actual settlement came from the military leaders who have no thought but to keep what they have got. The negotiations have been broken off. The Russian representatives were sincere and in earnest. They cannot entertain such proposals of conquest and domination.

The whole incident is full of significance. It is also full of perplexity. With whom are the Russian representatives dealing? For whom are the representatives of the Central Empires speaking? Are they speaking for the majorities of their respective parliaments or for the minority parties, that military and imperialistic minority which has so far dominated their whole policy and controlled the affairs of Turkey and of the Balkan States which have felt obliged to become their associates in this war?

The Russian representatives have insisted, very justly, very wisely, and in the true spirit of modern democracy, that the conferences they have been holding with the Teutonic and Turkish statesmen should be held within open, not closed, doors, and all the world has been audience, as was desired. To whom have we been listening, then? To those who speak the spirit and intention of the resolutions of the German Reichstag of the 9th of July last, the spirit and intention of the liberal leaders and parties of Germany, or to those who resist and defy that spirit and intention and insist upon conquest and subjugation? Or are we listening, in fact, to both, unreconciled and in open and hopeless contradiction? These are very serious and pregnant questions. Upon the answer to them depends the peace of the world.

But whatever the results of the parleys at Brest-Litovsk, whatever the confusions of counsel and of purpose in the utterances of the spokesmen of the Central Empires, they have again attempted to acquaint the world with their objects in the war and have again challenged their adversaries to say what their objects are and what sort of settlement they would deem just and satisfactory. There is no good reason why that challenge should not be responded to, and responded to with the utmost candour. We did not wait for it. Not once, but again and again we have laid our whole thought and purpose before the world, not in general terms only, but each time with sufficient definition to make it clear what sort of definite terms of settlement must necessarily spring out of them. Within the last week Mr Lloyd George has spoken with admirable candour and in admirable spirit for the people and Government of Great Britain.

There is no confusion of counsel among the adversaries of the Central Powers, no uncertainty of principle, no vagueness of detail. The only secrecy of counsel, the only lack of fearless frankness, the only failure to make definite statement of the objects of the war lies with Germany and her allies. The issues of life and death hang upon these definitions. No statesman who has the least conception of his responsibility ought for a moment to permit himself to continue this tragical and appalling outpouring of blood and treasure unless he is sure beyond a peradventure that the objects of the vital sacrifice are part and parcel of the very life of society and that the people for whom he speaks think them right and imperative as he does.

There is, moreover, a voice calling for these definitions of principle and of purpose which is, it seems to me, more thrilling and more compelling than any of the many moving voices with which the troubled air of the world is filled. It is the voice of the Russian people. They are prostrate and all but helpless, it would seem, before the grim power of Germany, which has hitherto known no relenting and no pity. Their power, apparently, is shattered. And yet their soul is not subservient. They will not yield either in principle or in action. Their conception of what is right, of what is humane and honourable for them to accept, has been stated with a frankness, a largeness of view, a generosity of spirit, and a universal human sympathy which must challenge the admiration of every friend of mankind; and they have refused to compound their ideals or desert others that they themselves may be safe.

They call to us to say what it is that we desire, in what, if in anything, our purpose and our spirit differ from theirs; and I believe that the people of the United States would wish me to respond, with utter simplicity and frankness. Whether their present leaders believe it or not, it is our heartfelt desire and hope that some way may be opened whereby we may be privileged to assist the people of Russia to attain their utmost hope of liberty and ordered peace.

It will be our wish and purpose that the processes of peace, when they are begun, shall be absolutely open and that they shall involve and permit henceforth no secret understandings of any kind. The day of conquest and aggrandizement is gone by; so is also the day of secret covenants entered into in the interest of particular governments and likely at some unlooked-for moment to upset the peace of the world. It is this happy fact, now clear to the view of every public man whose thoughts do not still linger in an age that is dead and gone, which makes it possible for every nation whose purposes are consistent with justice and the peace of the world to avow now or at any other time the objects it has in view.

We entered this war because violations of right had occurred which touched us to the quick and made the life of our own people impossible unless they were corrected and the world secured once for all against their recurrence.

What we demand in this war, therefore, is nothing peculiar to ourselves. It is that the world be made fit and safe to live in; and particularly that it be made safe for every peace-loving nation which, like our own, wishes to live its own life, determine its own institutions, be assured of justice and fair dealing by the other people of the world, as against force and selfish aggression.

All the people of the world are in effect partners in this interest, and for our own part we see very clearly that unless justice be done to others it will not be done to us.

The programme of the world's peace, therefore, is our programme; and that programme, the only possible programme, all we see it, is this:

1. Open covenants of peace must be arrived at, after which there will surely be no private international action or rulings of any kind, but diplomacy shall proceed always frankly and in the public view.

2. Absolute freedom of navigation upon the seas, outside territorial waters, alike in peace and in war, except as the seas may be closed in whole or in part by international action for the enforcement of international covenants.

3. The removal, so far as possible, of all economic barriers and the establishment of an equality of trade conditions among all the nations consenting to the peace and associating themselves for its maintenance.

4. Adequate guarantees given and taken that national armaments will be reduced to the lowest points consistent with domestic safety.

5. A free, open-minded, and absolutely impartial adjustment of all colonial claims, based upon a strict observance of the principle that in determining all such questions of sovereignty the interests of the population concerned must have equal weight with the equitable claims of the government whose title is to be determined.

6. The evacuation of all Russian territory and such a settlement of all questions affecting Russia as will secure the best and freest cooperation of the other nations of the world in obtaining for her an unhampered and unembarrassed opportunity for the independent determination of her own political development and

national policy, and assure her of a sincere welcome into the society of free nations under institutions of her own choosing; and, more than a welcome, assistance also of every kind that she may need and may herself desire. The treatment accorded Russia by her sister nations in the months to come will be the acid test of their good will, of their comprehension of her needs as distinguished from their own interests, and of their intelligent and unselfish sympathy.

7. Belgium, the whole world will agree, must be evacuated and restored, without any attempt to limit the sovereignty which she enjoys in common with all other free nations. No other single act will serve, as this will serve to restore confidence among the nations in the laws which they have themselves set and determined for the government of their relations with one another. Without this healing act the whole structure and validity of international law is forever impaired.

8. All French territory should be freed and the invaded portions restored, and the wrong done to France by Prussia in 1871 in the matter of Alsace-Lorraine, which has unsettled the peace of the world for nearly fifty years, should be righted, in order that peace may once more be made secure in the interest of all.

9. A readjustment of the frontiers of Italy should be effected along clearly recognizable lines of nationality.

10. The people of Austria-Hungary, whose place among the

nations we wish to see safeguarded and assured, should be accorded the freest opportunity of autonomous development.

11. Romania, Serbia, and Montenegro should be evacuated; occupied territories restored; Serbia accorded free and secure access to the sea; and the relations of the several Balkan states to one another determined by friendly counsel along historically established lines of allegiance and nationality; and international guarantees of the political and economic independence and territorial integrity of the several Balkan states should be entered into.

12. The Turkish portions of the present Ottoman Empire should be assured a secure sovereignty, but the other nationalities which are now under Turkish rule should be assured an undoubted security of life and an absolutely unmolested opportunity of autonomous development, and the Dardanelles should be permanently opened as a free passage to the ships and commerce of all nations under international guarantees.

13. An independent Polish state should be erected which should include the territories inhabited by indisputably Polish populations, which should be assured a free and secure access to the sea, and whose political and economic independence and territorial integrity should be guaranteed by international covenant.

14. A general association of nations must be formed under specific covenants for the purpose of affording mutual

guarantees of political independence and territorial integrity to great and small states alike.

In regard to these essential rectifications of wrong and assertions of right, we feel ourselves to be intimate partners of all the governments and people associated together against the imperialists. We cannot be separated in interest or divided in purpose. We stand together until the end.

Such arrangements and covenants we are willing to fight and to continue to fight until they are achieved; but only because we wish the right to prevail and desire a just and stable peace such as can be secured only by removing the chief provocations to war, which this programme does remove.

We have no jealousy of German greatness, and there is nothing in this programme that impairs it. We grudge her no achievement or distinction of learning or of pacific enterprise such as have made her record very bright and very enviable. We do not wish to injure her or to block in any way her legitimate influence or power. We do not wish to fight her either with arms or with hostile arrangements of trade, if she is willing to associate herself with us and the other peace-loving nations of the world in covenants of justice and law and fair dealing.

We wish her only to accept a place of equality among the people of the world—the new world in which we now live—instead of a place of mastery.

Neither do we presume to suggest to her any alteration

or modification of her institutions. But it is necessary, we must frankly say, and necessary as a preliminary to any intelligent dealings with her on our part, that we should know whom her spokesmen speak for when they speak to us, whether for the Reichstag majority or for the military party and the men whose creed is imperial domination.

We have spoken now, surely, in terms too concrete to admit of any further doubt or question. An evident principle runs through the whole programme I have outlined. It is the principle of justice to all people and nationalities, and their right to live on equal terms of liberty and safety with one another, whether they be strong or weak.

Unless this principle be made its foundation, no part of the structure of international justice can stand. The people of the United States could act upon no other principle, and to the vindication of this principle they are ready to devote their lives, their honour, and everything that they possess. The moral climax of this, the culminating and final war for human liberty has come, and they are ready to put their own strength, their own highest purpose, their own integrity and devotion to the test.

12

Winston Churchill

'We shall never surrender!'

∿

Churchill is a lone voice in questioning the country's policy of appeasement to Hitler.

Churchill Warns of Nazi Germany

London
16 November 1934

At present we lie within a few minutes' striking distance of the French, Dutch and Belgian coasts, and within a few hours of the great aerodromes of Central Europe. We are even within canon-shot of the Continent.

So close as that! Is it prudent, is it possible, however much we might desire it, to turn our backs upon Europe and ignore whatever may happen there? I have come to the conclusion—reluctantly I admit—that we cannot get away. Here we are and we must make the best of it. But do not underrate the risks—the grievous risks—we have to run.

◆

Just a few days after Chamberlain returned from Munich brandishing his now infamous scrap of paper, Churchill predicted that war had certainly not been averted. He was right.

Churchill's Speech on the Munich Agreement

House of Commons, London
5 October 1938

This is only the beginning of the reckoning. This is only the first sip, the first foretaste of a bitter cup which will be proffered to us year by year unless, by a supreme recovery of moral health and martial vigour, we arise again and take our stand for freedom as in the olden time.

◆

Chamberlain had resigned, and Churchill, then 65, had formed the government. His first speech in office settled the country's nerves.

First Speech as Prime Minister to House of Commons

House of Commons, London
13 May 1940

I would say to the House, as I said to those who have joined this government: I have nothing to offer but blood, toil, tears and sweat. We have before us an ordeal of the most grievous kind. We have before us many, many long months of struggle and of suffering. You ask, what is our policy? I can say: it is to wage war, by sea, land and air, with all our might and with all the strength that God can give us; to wage war against a monstrous tyranny, never surpassed in the dark, lamentable catalogue of human crime. This is our policy. You ask, what is our aim?

I can answer in one word: it is victory, victory at all costs, victory in spite of all terror, victory, however long and hard the road may be, for without victory, there is no survival.

◆

After the Dunkirk evacuation, Churchill calmed the nation's euphoria and stiffened its resolve.

Speech to Check the Mood of National Euphoria and Relief

House of Commons, London
4 June 1940

Even though large tracts of Europe and many old and famous states have fallen or may fall into the grip of the Gestapo and all the odious apparatus of Nazi rule, we shall not flag or fail. We shall go on to the end, we shall fight in France, we shall fight on the seas and oceans, we shall fight with growing confidence and growing strength in the air, we shall defend our island, whatever the cost may be, we shall fight on the beaches, we shall fight on the landing grounds, we shall fight in the fields and in the streets, we shall fight in the hills; we shall never surrender.

◆

Churchill stands tall in the face of an impending onslaught, and inspires the pilots of the RAF to victory in the Battle of Britain.

Battle of Britain Speech

House of Commons, London
18 June 1940

The battle of France is over. I expect that the Battle of Britain is about to begin. Upon this battle depends the survival of

Christian civilization. Upon it depends our own British life, and the long continuity of our institutions and our Empire. The whole fury and might of the enemy must very soon be turned upon us. Hitler knows that he will have to break us in this island or lose the war.

If we can stand up to him, all Europe may be free and the life of the world may move forward into broad, sunlit uplands. But if we fail, then the whole world, including the United States, including all that we have known and cared for, will sink into the abyss of a new Dark Age made more sinister, and perhaps more protracted, by the lights of perverted science. Let us therefore brace ourselves to our duties, and so bear ourselves that, if the British Empire and its Commonwealth last for a thousand years, men will still say, 'This was their finest hour.'

◆

As the Battle of Britain ended, Churchill praised the bravery of the R.A.F. pilots.

Speech about the R.A.F. Fighter Pilots

House of Commons, London
20 August 1940

The gratitude of every home in our Island, in our Empire, and indeed throughout the world, except in the abodes of the guilty, goes out to the British airmen who, undaunted by odds, unwearied in their constant challenge and mortal danger, are turning the tide of the World War by their prowess and by their devotion. Never in the field of human conflict was so much owed by so many to so few.

◆

Churchill warned about the threat of Soviet Russia. This stopped America's retreat into isolationism and led to the creation of NATO.

Iron Curtain Speech

Westminster College, Fulton, Missouri
5 March 1946

From Stettin in the Baltic to Trieste in the Adriatic, an iron curtain has descended across the Continent. Behind that line lie all the capitals of the ancient states of Central and Eastern Europe. Warsaw, Berlin, Prague, Vienna, Budapest, Belgrade, Bucharest and Sofia, all these famous cities and the populations around them lie in what I must call the Soviet sphere.

www.ingramcontent.com/pod-product-compliance
Lightning Source LLC
Chambersburg PA
CBHW032146020726
47496CB00003B/732